AF 112814

stories

Samir Sirk Morató

Copyright © 2026 by Samir Sirk Morató.

Front cover art ("dianoia ii") by Dusty Ray.

Typography, full cover wrap design,
and interior formatting by Alan Lastufka.

Interior art by Samir Sirk Morató.

All rights reserved.

No portion of this book may be reproduced in any form without
written permission from the publisher or author, except as
permitted by U.S. copyright law.

ISBN 979-8-9999212-2-2 (Paperback)
ISBN 979-8-9999212-3-9 (Ebook)

Praise for Gore Poetics

"Samir Sirk Morató's *Gore Poetics* burrows into the corpse of traditional horror fiction to emerge glistening with a new genre we might call 'lyrical splatter.' It's literary gristle laced with compassion, a feast of emotionally-charged body horror rooted and grown in the rotting true-crime landscape of the Midwestern US. Samir's stories refuse to find easy salvation, instead grinding their way into the light with equal scientific precision and earthiness. *Gore Poetics* is a powerful debut by a writer to watch and admire."

—**Joe Koch**, author of *The Wingspan of Severed Hands* and *Invaginies*

"*Gore Poetics* is incomparable. A sensuous and raw collection of stories where flesh reigns and the distinction between human and nature is corrupted with lyrical, elegiac prose. This is writing that thrives on our discomfort; in *Gore Poetics* we find both the truly repulsive but also, at their core, these are stories of great intimacy and tenderness. Morató seamlessly blends the two, thrusting us into strange worlds where everything is beautiful and everything hurts."
—**R.L. Summerling**

"Interviewed, David Cronenberg once said that everything but the body was abstract. With *Gore Poetics*, Samir Sirk Morató challenges that logic by making the body abstract. It is human flesh that is interchangeable as that of other natural and supranatural phylum—and acceptance, connection, and love ultimately as real as the body that yearns for it."
—**Karlo Yeager Rodríguez**

"This powerful debut collection explores what it is to be human, to have a body, and to be in connection with each other in all the visceral strangeness and alienation that those connections entail. These stories dazzle in abject brilliance, where boundaries blur, distort, and fracture into vivid tableaux of horror."

—**Tiffany Morris**, author of *Green Fuse Burning* and *Carnalis*

Contents

bluebell ovipositor	1
Colossus	9
The Halved World	21
LESS DEAD	39
sharp house	43
Lithopedion	51
EGREGORE	69
Poolhorse	79
limerence	85
PENNSYLVANIA FURNACE (Refrain)	91
Brainworms	103
famine frontier	119
Pearlescent Tickwad	123
galactic oracle eulogy	139
SHRIKE	145
dermestarium	165
Twilight Tide	175
entrada	193
Aberration	201
Acknowledgments	217
Publication History	219
About the Author	221
Content Guidelines	223
Other Releases from Cursed Morsels Press	225

Notice of Content Guidelines

Many stories in this collection deal with mature themes. A list of content guidelines is provided in the back of the book.

bluebell ovipositor

No one has ever seen Simone's fiancé, not in person or in photographs. Annecy doesn't care. When she stares at Simone's engagement-ringed finger she's imagining it inside her. Not the void who's marrying Simone.

"Annecy, darling, you should really find someone."

Simone's lips are against Annecy's ear under the pretense of discussing entomology. The slit of her dress is riding against Annecy's wheelchair arm. Her skin is a breath from Annecy's. They sit nestled in the cervix of a dilapidated auditorium, lights dim, their professor droning about oviposition, the projector casting images of grasshopper underbelly, pink tube, and loam thrust aside for eggs onto an aged, velvety screen.

Annecy coughs so she doesn't shudder. She grips her chair's wheels. "Finding someone isn't a problem. Everything else is."

"It shouldn't be, if you work things right."

The murk disguises Simone's emaciation. The hollow of her collar seems less severe, her hips less sunken. It does for her appearance what her drench of bluebell perfume does for her smell: it masks whatever the sabbatical did to her. She's almost the woman Annecy met last spring semester.

Simone's hand creeps upwards. It fingers the waist of Annecy's skirt.

"Lavender is a lovely color," she murmurs. "A practical one. I'm having a lavender wedding. You should too. It'd suit you."

Annecy starts praying the pool between her legs dries before they leave the accommodating dark and reenter the harsh, well-lit world. She can't focus on Simone's innuendo-warning with her smell right there. It's crawling into her mouth. Probing her nostrils. The odor under the bluebell is wet: near rank. It's umami. Annecy cannot tell if it comes from a hole that should be seeping or a seeping hole that shouldn't exist. She wants to be afraid.

The grasshopper, eyes black, is rhythmically pulsing her abdomen into the ground. *Even the severed abdomen,* the professor is saying, *will continue these movements. As long as the female is sexually mature...*

"You should come to my apartment," Simone says.

"What about your fiancé?"

"What about him?"

Annecy knows every clothed curve of Simone's breasts and while there's something off in the way they fill her dress, some broken mathematical rule she cannot place, her windpipe tightens around the hot, sharp realization that there's a protrusion around Simone's nipple. Maybe a barbell. It and the invitation to intimacy are new.

"Here's my address." Simone takes the pen hanging from Annecy's blouse. She reaches beneath Annecy's arms, sleeve nudging against raised hair, to write her address onto a notebook. Annecy exhales when she withdraws.

The professor has moved on to reproductive parasitism

now. Different ways of birthing slick eggs; different crevices to shove them into.

"See you later," Simone says. She gathers her things then leaves.

Annecy splutters. It's weak. She stares at Simone's cursive, processing its cramped, conjoined letters, her body aching while a projected mud dauber pumps eggs onto a spider, before she realizes that Simone—unlike in past lectures—took no other notes at all.

She beats off more times per day than she attends class. She sits alone in entomology for weeks. No one has seen Simone, but they shrug off Annecy's questions with *She's getting married, isn't she? Maybe that's why,* as if Simone's partner penetrates not just her but her schooling, her schedule, her every choice. The absences and distortions once excused by 'busy with dating' and 'busy with engagement' have metamorphosed into marriage and outright disappearance.

It's such a natural transition that it unnerves Annecy more than it enrages her. When does suspicion crystallize into terror? If no one cares, if no one pays attention, when does a chrysalis become a grave instead of a changing place? Annecy cannot bear the thought of her health being governed by a man's shadow, though it already is. She fills herself with fingers and toys so there's one less spot for dread to enter.

When waiting becomes too much to bear, Annecy takes a cane and buses to Simone's apartment complex. She suspects it won't be chair-accessible. She's correct: the complex's ancient doors are heavy, its stairs steep. All its wiring and livability are afterthoughts. Annecy trudges through hallways pitted with stagnant units, warped railings, and peeling common spaces. By the time she reaches Simone's apartment, fall bruises splotch her legs.

Her knocks go unanswered. Annecy almost falls again when she tries the knob and the door swings inward. It slams behind her once she's in. The apartment is a murky squeeze of chambers: a protrusion into the complex's walls. Low buzzing rattles its vents. Once she gropes through the kitchen, Annecy can see down the apartment's length.

Simone is standing naked in the living room.

Naked of everything. She's a near skeleton. A juicy, fetid matrix throbbing with enormous maggots. They crowd each other in her cavities in lieu of offal, their spiracles entangled in the adipose-flesh slush left, pudgy fingers forced through rotting hymen. They're sucking at the spine. When Simone pirouettes to look at Annecy, flesh rags dangle from her bone in fringe. Her face is paler than her cleaned femurs. Simone smiles. The carpet between her feet is wet. It comes from the crowning maggot above.

"Hello, Annecy. I'm glad you finally visited!"

Annecy hears the crash of herself hitting her knees. She white knuckle grips her cane as Simone coos at her maggots. They trade holes. Their girth swells and ebbs, segment by segment, as they locomate around the host-slick. Some are bristly. Developing wings and pliable legs.

"This is nothing a wedding dress can't cover." Simone poses. "Now, regardless of what fails, I'll never die. I'm within my children."

"How could this happen? Your fiancé—"

"He picked this apartment."

A maggot reclines on Simone's chest, swaddled in what's left of her breast skin. It works its mouth-hooks around her nipple from inside her as if it's chewing a pacifier. They glimmer. Uterine rot and humidity born from body fluids blankets Annecy. It oozes into her skin. She salivates in an involuntary attempt to expel it from her sinuses, from her; drool strings down her chin and onto her knees.

Something is thumping inside a distant wall.

"I see myself in you, you know," Simone says. "I was in your position before. We're obligated to get married and produce children, yet that means men. It's awful."

The thumping is at the closed bedroom door. It's accompanied by buzzing that vibrates into Annecy's core. She sobs. A fruity stench settles over all the stained, torn furniture.

"I did the impossible, darling." Simone's head floats above the raw, fucked nursery of her body. "I built a traditional family without a man. Do you want to meet my fiancé?"

"No," Annecy cries. But the door is already opening to reveal the stranger behind it, the wasp-waisted tower of antennae, segments, and lacy wings, the presence whose womb-lance made this possible. The maggots are crying not quite like babies. Simone is setting water glasses on what's left of a table. Her fiancé looms. Annecy becomes aware of her own existing holes: her five million pores, her dripping mucous membranes, her lavender predicament.

What's a few more? What's a curse for freedom?

That microfilament of a thought opens her. Its intrusiveness doesn't matter. An entrance is an entrance. It's not Simone's finger inside Annecy. Not her engagement ring. Annecy whines around the feeler probing her. It tents the inside of her cheek. It fingers her palate with all the tentativeness of revelation, inviting, repulsive. Annecy can't breathe. She never could. The feeler frots her tongue, as moist and ridged as inverted internal membrane, rank, demure only in comparison to the gown-gallows that awaits.

There's never been comparison before.

Simone will never regain what she's traded away. Does that matter? Flesh rots while lace unravels; eggs hatch; there's no unmarrying in the way that matters, but Simone has supplanted the nightmare planned for her. That alternative thrums inside Annecy's mouth. Agency, when sucked from its moldy casing, is cadaverously sweet.

Annecy trembles. She slackens her jaw. The feeler, slick with her drool, slides in quickly. Annecy moans. Her throat spreads for it, making room for new ambitions, forms, and once unvoiceable things. Simone, core writhing, is folding mildewy napkins while she talks about introducing Annecy to her fiancé's friends.

It's easy, she's saying. Once you let it in, it's easy. You don't lose what matters. You don't lose anything at all.

Colossus

My grandfather died alone and afraid. Neither are surprising. He lived alone because he was afraid; he died in fear because he was alone. Some would argue that he died in company, but I know better. You are still alone when the thing calling is yourself. I also know this: I am stronger than my grandfather. Despite all his decades, he never understood that the best gifts arrive with agony.

No one gave Grandfather's house to me. That doesn't matter. Who's going to evict me? I eat an apple on his porch while winter afternoon breaks on the prairie. My first bite almost fills me. As a connoisseur of starvation, I don't need much. I never do.

Afternoon comes in waves of gray, heavy light that oppress the eternity of grass. Lines of barbed wire fences and buck-and-rail snow guards crisscross the grassland for miles. Once they're distant enough, they resemble stitches crawling across a scalp. Everything smells of sage and high-desert death. The sky, so wide it triggers weeping, makes it clear that there's nowhere to hide.

My grandfather moved outside Laramie to avoid socializing. Perhaps to avoid progress, too. The nearest neighbor is so far they're invisible, the nearest grocery store an hour's drive. Pronghorn use the roads here as much as people. The rest of the family would rather deepthroat a shotgun than live out here, particularly after the funeral. I think it suits me.

A flock of longspurs skim the yard, shaking frost off the grass. A breeze chases after them. It nips my numbing fingertips. I eat another bite. When the wind stays slow and carries nothing but the sound of rustling grass, I throw the rest of the apple into the grass. I retreat inside. I am not sulking when I slam the door.

Grandfather's house overflows with threadbare carpet, antler lamps worn with touch, and mouse-eaten furniture. Signs of rituals undertaken in a tiny universe. I don't care about the old man's sentimentalities. I beeline for the place that matters: his bedroom. My bedroom. I savor the cold creeping through the hardwood. It stings my bare feet. During the demon hours, its frigidity is punishing. I relish knowing winter will deepen its bite.

The ancient wallpaper, whorls of navy ivy carpeting eggshell blue, is intact. So is the wall of words that squirms across it from ceiling to floor. *Oh the wind winnows,* my grandfather's cursive says. *Oh the wind winnows.* Again, and again, written thousands of times, crawling together without punctuation or pause. Grandfather's only will. It creates a current of its own. The marker he wrote it with is worn silver with use, its label erased.

I stare at his words from the foot of the bed. They hunger me in a way I am not used to. I cannot let this avenue go unexplored. Since Grandfather is dead, they've cut the electricity off. His bedside kerosene lamp is dim. In the murk, I strip, then fold my arms above my head. I flex before the windows. With the blinds back, my reflection is all periwinkle ribs, jutting hips, and concave stomach. I am so deliciously close to disappearing. Instead of studying myself and ruining my joy, I read spirals of prose until my eyes strain.

The house groans.

* * *

Laramie is a man-made wind tunnel.

That fact always throws tourists. Sometimes it throws locals. Not that Laramie has ever been windless. Before men took a whetstone to the knife already at their throats, forests of bristlecone pines—gnarled by altitude, contorted by wind—spiked the nearby mountainsides. They still do. Those terrible little trees have been mummifying for two centuries. From their hospices, they rattle in the wind, so changed by its rage that they've corkscrewed to withstand it, so embittered that their remaining bark shrieks in joy as gales rip through it on their way to ravage the plains.

During windiest months, gusts running a minimum of twelve mph fly in. The prairies see a minimum of nearly sixteen.

Maybe it was less before. Everything worsened when settlers logged the trees around town. Bit by bit, they eroded their protection. Bit by bit, they let the wolf in. I understand their reasoning. Before, I believed in excess. Blooming big seemed like it would permit me to fill space. But I was so small and singular, and the prairies were so vast. Filling them—even filling Laramie—was an impossible task. Still, as a superior monstrosity, I believed myself capable. I gorged on buffet food until my presence expanded. I shopped until bags of clothes entombed my apartment. I slept my way through the city's twenty-seven bars, smoking packs between hook-ups, cutting lines before, cutting my thighs afterwards, contemptuous that my marks—human and razor—thought I desired them. This was about me.

I indulged until it landed me in the hospital. When charcoal purged my system, I realized the answer was restraint. Less is more. Now I, too, have shaved away excess in the pursuit of fuel and aesthetics. What emerges from the wind tunnel and I is sharper. Harsher. We cannot help what results from fasting.

On one cataclysmic day, the mountains saw a 128 mph windstorm.

Before it took him, Grandfather said the wind was calling his name. He told me that while we encountered each other outside Ridley's last month. The anxiety I'd seen brewing over autumn had been boiling, then. He'd licked his lips every other word. Clung to his bag of celery and sausage with trembling, near translucent hands. The way his clothes engulfed him indicated that he was a creature on the verge of obsolescence, and instead of embracing what annihilation had to teach him, he'd chosen to cower.

"_____," he'd said, his cheekbones sunken, tongue working at his dentures, arthritic legs trembling. "God, it's good to see you. It's good to see anyone. I can't have anyone out at the house with the wind out there. Not with it talking. Calling me. I'm afraid of what it'd do. I'm afraid your ma would put me in a home if I told her. I'm plumb afraid. You ain't going to tell her, are you?"

And I, riding high on a breakfast of cigarettes and four saltines, having not spoken to Mom in months, admired his emaciation and said, "Of course not, Grandpa."

They found his remains tangled in a barbed wire fence two weeks later.

The family wanted a closed casket funeral. Of course they did. Propriety is the enemy of honesty. I peeked into the coffin before the funeral began. I cannot describe how my grandfather looked beyond that he was *gone*. A handful of flesh ligated together into human scaffolding. The Great Depression as a body.

Colossus

Later, as sandwiches, tea, and watery chatter littered the wake, I sat in the back, stunned, envious longing gnawing through me. I knew then that I had to experience what Grandfather had. To live even more leanly.

Grandfather died three months ago. I've been camping here for three days, hoping the wind will call.

* * *

The next fourteen days are the same.

Each morning begins with a cup of coffee, a cup of water, two out of six daily apple slices, and renewed efforts at seduction. I utilize identical tactics every day. While the desolate prairie ripples, I try to coax the wind in by feigning disinterest. This is phase one. I stack Grandfather's table high with his books about the ocean and pretend to gasp in fear. I chew my nails at photos of submarines; I moan at images of deep sea beasts, sometimes shaking my head in disgust.

Privately, I don't understand why my grandfather abandoned his cushy seaside home for us in Wyoming. When he arrived, I was too young to visit him and too old to love him, not that I've ever loved anyone. He was too fragile for the elements. He should've stayed in Florida, with his zephyrs and beaches. Thalassophobia and philia are for hedonists. Those don't grow here.

When a couple hours of jealousy-baiting doesn't work, I eat two more apple slices, then shift gears. Time for the second phase: imitating vulnerability. I peek outside. If the wind is gentle, I open the door further. If it accelerates, I duck back inside. Any acting challenge is welcome to me. Once the wind picks up, per usual, I pretend to fortify against it. I imitate my grandfather's fitful pacing and glancing until coffee cleanses my guts, return from the bathroom, and pace again. I lock and unlock windows, as if saying

Just to be sure! I stuff towels in any unstuffed niches. I peer between blinds.

During all this, I make a show of layering on clothes. Leggings and a shirt go on first thing in the morning. By ten, a jacket and socks have joined. By eleven, there's gloves and a beanie. At noon, when I eat my fifth and sixth apple slices, I add sweats over the leggings. When cigarette dinner arrives, I'm a swollen beast of warmers, scarves, socks, and outer layers. A monster wallowing about and commenting on their dwindling stack of firewood as their own sweat pickles them. All in hopes that the wind will smell fake fear and take interest in me.

It's pitiable that once sundown happens, once my reflection shows more crisply, I can't ever stand my bloated outline. I shuck my layers. Without fail, I tear the blinds from a window. I behold myself in the glass, flushed, always begging to be thinner than I am. The wind never ceases combing through the prairie. I'm sure it sees me floundering. It laughs. By midnight, I slink to bed.

Outside of the wind, I don't know whose approval I want. Whose gazes I'm aiming to please. Other people have never interested me. They're boring. They're tasteless. I sicken when I feel their gazes on me anyway. Are they judging me? Do they find me disgusting? What parts of me are misshapen? How can I fix them? All that anxiety diminishes me. Sometimes, I'm no different than my grandfather. Maybe he had the right idea by isolating himself.

That thought halts others. It always comes back to me. I hate humanity more than anything in the world. I am also superior to everyone else, so hating my pathetic self takes priority over hating people. That also means that my body is the body. Whatever I craft it into is a pinnacle. I remind myself of that while I'm crying into the pillows. Grandfather's ivy-tangled mantra surrounds me.

Another day, another failure. All that's left is trying again.

* * *

Day eighteen is different.

I wake up imagining the 128 mph squall. How it must've felt on the skin. On the exposed nerves. As hours pass, I eat my bag of popcorn, taking it slow so my belly won't bulge. No reading today. No charade of fortification. Jackrabbits stare while I pour boiling coffee into my mouth. It splatters the porch when I cough it up. The jackrabbits flee. All I want is a taste of annihilation. Of what it means to be stripped clean by the un-withstandable.

The sun glares at the prairie. It scorches, even with clouds coming in. A celestial panopticon. I walk circles around the house, naked, wheatgrass and junegrass needling my soles. Mice flee underfoot. How stupid they are, forever sneaking inside for gulps of polyester or uncooked rice, refusing the gift of scarcity offered to them out here. The temperature falls. Cold rakes my burnt throat. I hear my rhythmic wheezing. My toes numb. Sagebrush carries ripples for miles as a breeze shoots through. It drizzles.

"You don't understand," I croak into the wind. "I need you. Call me the way you called my grandfather. You think you're good at winnowing? Fuck you! No one winnows like me."

The wind intensifies; the rain tilts. Becomes sleet arrows pinging my flesh. Chill blanches my body.

"Are you afraid?" I wave. "Oh, poor little wind, not used to being called first. I won't bite."

My skin is gooseflesh. Grass whips my legs until blood beads them. A shriek builds in my ear drums. Knives of cold slice at my pelvis, ribs, and chest. Then, in a rattle of barbed wire, all quiets. My breath catches.

"Wait. Don't leave," I say. "Please don't leave."

When the wind returns it says my name. First in a whisper. Then, as the house shakes, in a howl.

* * *

I cry first.

I can't help it. My hair whips back so hard that it yanks at my head, makes me feel like grasping hands are scalping me, but the tears are constant. The wind blasts water out of my eyes. I stumble through the prairie, ever-replenishing wet streaks chilling my face, lips peeled, gums stinging, teeth white with sleet, nothing against me or in me but windscream. The house is a dot. Then it's gone. It's me and the vast nothing cut by fences. There's too much air to breathe. Every exhale is torn free before it's born and beaten on rocks.

When I fall, I roll, then crawl, then stagger, but I do not stop. Wind forces me onward. Rocks chew my knees and elbows. Skin dangles from them in pieces. Cow shit and tumbleweed tangle my hair. My heartbeat whines low in my chest. Snow gnaws at my bloody feet. Packs itself into the warm crevices before crystalizing. I am aflame with cold.

"This isn't too bad." I gasp, my mouth blisters broken by twigs, their fluid dribbling from my lips alongside drool. "Do better."

I know the wind hears me when broken longspurs rain from the sky.

It catches me like a doll. Throws me forward. Drags me. I am sprinting, then, as fast as I ever have, my vision throbbing red, my lungs heaving, muscles shaking, until the effort is out of my hands. My strides grow longer, and longer, beyond the stretch of my body. I skate on the prairie. Grass grates the soles of my feet off. When they hit meat, that too grates away. Then bone. The agony is too beautifully constant to scream.

We fly, and fly, and fly, over miles, over fences, until 'over' isn't an option. The spines of a buck-and-rail fence hurtle closer. Closer. Too close. The wind hurls me into a section of it. Snow explodes, timbers crack; my lower back snaps. While tangled in the fence, I look back at miles of parallel steaming, scarlet lines. Everything below my knobbly ankles is gone.

The wind veers off. I sneak a trembling inhale. Endless sky and endless plains are the same. I cannot even see where the Rockies break them. Everything is white. I hear the wind returning before I feel it: it's a skitter of sleet. Gravel. A storm gaining speed as it barrels over an eternity of rolling hills. Oh, my name! My name, my name, my name!

It hits.

Gravel, sleet, and ice sandblast me at what must be hurricane strength. They drive into me. All I can comprehend are the minute rocks studding my face like strawberry seed pits. The wind needles into every puncture it's made. I am unchanged. I am nothing but holes. Ten thousand budding wind tunnels. With a squelch, my scalp flies free.

My lips begin disappearing first. Then my pitted cheeks. The wind eats them away. My nose shaves lower. My ears. Nipples go, then nails. I register that my thigh gap nearly extends from femur to femur when a crushed bucket flies between my legs. My skin, exfoliated to ruin, sloughs off. With it goes my nerves. My muscle bares itself to the world. I am now free. I scream back into the wind as it whittles holes through me and my membranes. When the wind pierces through, they whistle like fishing pole eyelets in a gale.

Wind punctures eyes. Punctures organs. Steals liquid from anything that holds it and unspools tendons from any place they thread. Viscera icicles spray the snow before the drifts vanish. This is how metal under an oxy acetylene torch feels: it liquifies beneath heat before air blows it away. The belief that heat and cold differ is wrong. I am screaming even when I am lungless, even when my limbs rip off, hurtle between slats in the fence, and tumble across the prairie. Even when their rolling grinds them to nothing too. Even when I am spread thin across the torqued bodies of bristlecone pines.

Oh, how the wind winnows! I am particles on wingtips yet wider than the world itself. A colossus full of hunger; an atom free of size. It's all I've ever wanted.

I don't even mind feeling it all.

The Halved World

Your Friday starts tits up. The goons at the grocery store keep making cracks about how if you're back here bagging milk pints and condoms *something* must have gone wrong the two years you spent away. Then Frankie Hartnell pretends not to know you when you call out to her during a parking lot cigarette break, and before closing, your manager tells you he's cutting your hours. You bike the exhaust-choked fifty minutes back to your trailer, fuming.

It's so fucking stupid, you think, cards whirring in your spokes, wind fingering the holes in your jacket. The flashlight jerry-rigged onto your handlebars splutters. *Is this punishment because I skipped town? God.*

Entropy came home before you. Twilight peers through your blinds in broken slats. Fly cadavers blacken the strips noosing the kitchen. The floorboards groan before puffing a cologne sample of rot wherever you walk. You try to enjoy your can of musty vienna sausages in peace. The house key beside your hand is worn with use, but your fingerprints alone cloud the doorknob and screen latch.

When you finally yank on gloves and go to weed the

furthest back plot of your garden, you see it behind the high weeds: the duplicate of you nude and prostrate in the soil, eyes open, mouth slack, a snail nibbling at its tongue, navel still attached to a vine.

You groan.

*　*　*

It's easier to deal with these things once you've caught them early. Oftentimes, fruit flourishes best in hiding. You clip your umbilical cord with hedge clippers and heave your lookalike into the wheelbarrow. Its side is misshapen from pressing into the dirt without proper rotation; its weight is off. You should have found and pruned this shit a year ago. That's what procrastination gets you.

Normally, your family would yank on their rubber boots, wheelbarrow all the unwanted additions to the concrete slab in the back, chop them into sections with cleavers, and add them to the crypt below the floor to compost. That seemed so effortless when you were a kid. Alone, handling even one crop is hard work. You're the last of the Woodwards maintaining the plot, the final family gardener, and the era of harvests is gone.

You're huffing as you roll your lookalike onto the grass by the water hose. Dicing it seems awful while you're so alone. Instead, you investigate all its orifices to make sure it didn't bring in any hitchhikers before spraying it clean. It watches you from the stairs while you crush all the flushed snails with your boot.

After that, you polish it with a rag and cart it into your room. You heave it onto the spare twin bed across from you. The bare mattress creaks under the weight of two yous. *Dud,* you think, feeling your lookalike's corn silk hair and rind-hard ankles and wrists. This other self never ripened. There may be a pocket of flesh or two languishing in its core, but realization was out of the question before you picked it.

You drape a towel over its underdeveloped chest. Seeing yourself exposed without baggy clothes brings discomfort. Then you dig out your shortbread tin of weed and head downstairs to the phone.

The curls of the phone wire hang thick with dust as you dial up one of your cousins again. All the ancient almanac calendars, lopsided furniture, and dessicated seed packets magnet-pinned to the fridge haven't shifted a centimeter since you were five years old. They disintegrate in place.

The pin-up posters streaking the walls with painted tits and thighs are yours, as is the dart board, but they retain a dried quality. You hung them before you left. Nothing has swayed them since.

You light a joint as the call rolls to the answering machine.

"Hey, asshole," you say, jabbing an entry in the withered contact book, "I found a huge lookalike behind the house today. Christ knows how that thing isn't ripe. We're lucky it was a bad crop. What's wrong with y'all? No one has done jackshit to keep the garden in shape. One of you has gotta help me. Call me back. I mean it."

You hang up, exhale a cloud, then punch in the next series of numbers in the phone book. Five disconnected numbers in, you ash your joint. No one's personal information is current. Come to think of it, do you know where any of your fifteen cousins live anymore?

You chew on the roach, highly heartsick, when you dial Frankie Harnell's number for good measure. Each time, the call goes through before clicking off.

After three dials you put your head on the table.

* * *

You're checking out the items for a fried thirty-something with a baby on her waist and a curl of perm foil in her up-do, shoveling cups of cling peaches, diaper packages, and nicotine patches into plastic bags, when your shitty coworkers start arguing about the National Enquirer headlines. The one with long hair shoots you a sneaky glance.

"I don't know nothing about how a flying saucer works," he says, "but I bet Mister Community College over here could explain it to us."

"I didn't get an associate's degree in flying saucers," you say.

"Course not." He nods at you. "You spent two years getting one in..."

"Welding."

The thirty-something jitters her leg and flips through the personal ads. You ignore her turnipesque baby.

"Must not be too many welding jobs outside of Piper's Gap," Long Hair says.

"Reckon not."

"That's a shame, since you've got the degree and everything."

"Yeah."

"My mom's looking for a welder." Glasses Boy chimes in from the side. Long Hair grins as you punch open the cash register and give the thirty-something her change.

"I'll talk to your mom later," you say, longing to spit *when she's blowing me* but too scared of what the grocery goons will discuss if you do. The baby shrieks.

Long Hair almost snickers.

* * *

From where you sit in your room, you can see out your window to the dark, new pavement on the road. It's almost hidden by the waist-deep grass that rustles around your house.

"That road used to be full of potholes," you inform your lookalike, loading a bowl. "You can drive on it without killing your suspension now. I don't know when that happened. I don't know when anyone got the money to do that."

Your lookalike doesn't flinch when you blow a bong rip at them. You study the curves of its distorted body—the Woodward body. The lookalike's nudity is natural. It's like purveying a squash in a bowl. You're unsure why your own body seems so rotten and wrong. It's not uglier than your lookalike.

The clipped umbilical cord has become a stem. It protrudes from the lookalike's navel, horn-like. A vine ringlet hangs from its top and drapes onto the lookalike's pelvis. You don't touch your lookalike's ripe stretches until you've smoked your bowl. With your mouth dry and fingers tingling, you stroke your lookalike's ribs.

The skin is fuzzy. Room temperature. You stroke the ribs again before reaching for the face. Parts are unripe, here, hard and malformed. The nose is sunken, the cartilage green. You pet the dandelion fluff eyebrows before rolling the lookalike's lip up under your thumb. As expected, empty gums greet you. A handful of pumpkin seed teeth protrude in the front. You don't need to pluck one to know they're rubbery.

"You're as ugly as some of the little bastards outside," you say.

The lookalike sits unmoving in its dented spiderweb. You set your bong down and lean in. No breath brushes your cheeks. The lashes smell of lavender. You rip them out in clumps and pack them into your bowl.

"We're stuck." You watch the grass sway outside. "You're us, but worse. I'm me. There ain't much either of us can do."

When you're relaxed, you jam a jar between your lookalike's stiff thighs, then feed the umbilical into its aspirin-laced water. No point in letting it rot early.

* * *

"Lord, you're one of the Woodwards, aren't you?"

The old man with glasses thicker than spit squints. His arthritic claws stay clamped around his coupons. You scan his newspaper, denture cleaner, and ginseng pills.

"Guilty as charged," you say. "I'm the tenth one."

The old man waves. "The tenth one? Christ almighty. Half the town's a Woodward. 'Til recently, none of 'em left Piper's Gap through nothing but the courthouse."

Your teeth grind.

"I've been out," you say. "Went to community college and everything. I almost moved to Clifton Forge, after I graduated, but the trailer—"

"You've all got the same look about you," the old man says. "All you Woodwards. Lots of funky teeth and fine, fine hair. You're all cousins too, ain'tcha? I've never seen a Woodward senior."

"Yeah." His receipt rips in your grip. "We are."

The old man's daughter, a middle-aged bruiser that's more piercings than skin, raps on the window, her truck idling. "Come on," she mouths. He gives you a paternal warning look.

"Be good, now," the old man says. "Ma'am. Sir. Whichever one. That don't matter. A Woodward is a Woodward."

Go fuck yourself.

You smile. "Have a nice day."

* * *

While you ponder where the old waterpark went and when the library moved, you prune the garden. Most families have a tree. Yours has a vine. You crawl beneath the noon sun, taking stock of what grows on the vine's winding, greedy tendrils. The ragged leaves. The tissuey blossoms. The embryonic scallop squashes. Green filigree ensnares the yard, pulsing with sickly life.

You stand there at the root of your family's genesis, two shoplifted Fudgesicles chilling your guts, an electricity bill chilling your heart, thistle stings burning your hands. Disgruntlement sets in. You don't know when cultivating the next generation became a chore. The tasks haven't changed, but all awe has fled. The lookalikes are annoying vegetables; maintaining the Woodward vine means nothing but weeding and spreading cow shit around.

No wonder everyone dumped this on me, you think. *No one enjoys nasty work.*

Two of the embryonic squashes, no bigger than your fist, fared poorly last night. One's head was eaten halfway through by a deer. Another's punctured belly swarms with beetles. Their bulging eyes are knots, their mouths deadend indentations. They gnarl into themselves as they dangle from the vine. It's too early for their pseudo-fetal shapes to have Woodward features. In several months, they would have begun manifesting.

You snap the embryos free, chop them in half, and hurl them into a bucket, pitted innards and all. Lookalikes don't suffer. You can't empathize with that anymore. Realization means agony. Even if lookalikes did feel pain, the town doesn't want more Woodwards. Your selectivity does everyone a favor.

God knows your cousins don't do favors anymore. All this is on you.

You soak rags in your lookalike's damp mouth to replace the fly strips you can't afford as you dial your unresponsive family again, crying out more than greeting them, even when confused strangers answer your calls that go through.

* * *

"Mom says you haven't asked her about the job yet," Glasses Boy says.

"Blow me."

You slash at another pile of boxes with your box cutter. The stench of weed wafts into your hoodie. Glasses Boy smirks. Helpless rage makes your peripheral vision a mirage.

"Pretty sure that won't teach you how to weld," Glasses Boy says. "Think you participated in enough blow jobs the last two years anyhow, depending on where they put you."

"I'm going to the register," you mutter. "You can handle all this."

"You sure you want to, smelling like that? If the sheriff comes back in here again it'd be bad news."

It's impossible to tell if concern or mockery glitters in Glasses Boy's expression. You tear into another box. Soon enough, you're alone in the backroom.

* * *

"You're a fuck-up," you hiss at the vegetable in your room, grinding your spliff into its wrist again. "You know that?"

The lit end sizzles against the lookalike's peel. It leaves a fifth blistered circle. Its newly zip-tied wrists glow with charred spots. Despite all the crushed aspirin and water changes, the lookalike is rotting. Fingernails lengthen as its skin recedes; its hair mimics growth as its scalp shrinks. The zip ties cuffing the lookalike's ankles peer half-visible from their canals in the skin. Flies crawl on your sweating wallpaper.

"You never get anything right." You can't choose between fuming or crying. "Fucking hell."

You opt to rekindle your spliff's cherry with another puff and jab again.

When you stumble out back, spent, you sink to your knees among the family vine. Its latticework of purple veins throb with sap. You see double the veins and double the hungry, reaching leaves as your vision comes undone. Slugs, remembering past meals, slither towards you before turning away. Katydids stumble through your leg hair.

I want a machete, you think. Then: *Why?* What would you do with it? Ridding yourself of this legacy, somehow, is as unfathomable as quitting your job.

You sit outside until cricketsong calls the dark home.

The rat-tail adorned creep in a hoodie scratches at his mustache, if that waterline mark of hair can be called a mustache. You ring up the third bottle of robitussin he's come in to buy this week instead of making eye contact. His gaze burns into your name tag as you bag a bottle of lube, mentos, and a whipped cream canister.

"Hey!" he says. "I used to see you around here."

You grunt. "I've worked here a long time."

"Didn't you work with Frankie at that sheet cake place?"

Bile splashes up into your throat.

"No," you say. "I'm Frankie's best friend. Have been since ninth grade."

"Huh. I mean, I saw you two together all the time, but Frankie looked grouchy, and you don't really lounge around a cake place 24/7 'less you've got a reason to be there. So I assumed—"

"Frankie has a resting bitch face," you say.

"I don't think so." The creep frowns. "Her resting face looks pretty bored. At least before she sees me."

You want to strangle him. Your self doubt leashes you. "Your total is $15.75," you say. "Anything else?"

The creep wipes his runny nose. "If you didn't get put away for something violent, and that big ole hoodie isn't too loose on you uptop, I, uh, need your number."

"Go back to doing whippets in study hall, asshole," you say.

The creep pays in sweaty bills and coins before slinking out the door. Your coworkers burst into laughter. You rip apart the creep's receipt, boiling. You wish Frankie Hartnell was here to defend the mutuality of your friendship. You aren't sure she would. Did all that borrowed money and bummed rides to school mean friendship, or was that just proximity? Frankie didn't live far from you. Her family hired yours for odd jobs. Maybe obligation is proximity's neighbor. While you're restocking milk, you try to imagine Frankie's resting expression. Nothing but blurred features clutter your brain.

You know even less about your best friend than you know about yourself.

* * *

One of the older propagations who's ghosting you said *You are what you imbibe.*

He was smart, in the ubiquitous Woodward way. Still is, unless you've missed another death. You bet your fillings he escaped Piper's Gap after you. Maybe he tricked some middle-class girl into marriage. That would be a hard sell, since none of you have the equipment for spousal duties or creating children, but Woodwards excel at rooting in hostile ground.

Your cousin meant his comment in the sense of flesh

consuming flesh, of what separates lookalikes and people, but you hope that consuming yourself will get you closer to who you are.

You lean over your lookalike as you flick open your box cutter. The fact this botanic miscarriage shifts at night while it sinks into the mattress means your time is limited. Soon, it'll be fertilizer.

The blade shakes when you puncture the lookalike's side. There's a pop. At once, your tension flees. It feels no different than cutting a zucchini. You slice a square into the lookalike's unmoving abdomen, fumble, then peel the pane of skin free.

The skin unsuckers from the body. The muscle underneath is the color and texture of milkweed stem: white, wet. Seepage comes, but no blood. Your lip curls as you set the peel aside to dry for rolling paper.

Every day, you remember this thing isn't fully realized. You aren't either, but you're made of named meat, which puts you damn well above this gourd. It pays no rent; it wears no worries. It reclines in decaying repose at your mercy and burdens you.

"You could've been worth something," you tell it, knowing it cannot hear you crying in your adjacent twin bed at night. "Not anymore."

Its lashless eyes stare ceilingward, its bound wrists making its posture meek.

* * *

Mrs. Pryor has three bottles of black hair dye, migraine medication, and one apple in her basket. You're so sick with joy to see her that you overlook Glasses Boy ringing up Frankie Hartnell an aisle over. Not that Frankie or Mrs. Pryor is too close to you.

"Mrs. Pryor!" you say. "Long time no see!"

She starts. Her eyes are watery. The tote she's slotted into the bag carousel wilts. Mrs. Pryor always looked unsteady compared to her volleyball-spiking daughter. She looks ready to collapse now.

"Goodness," she says. "Is that who I think it is?"

"In the flesh." You vibrate. "How are you? How's Abilene? I haven't seen her since graduation! Did she end up moving to Blacksburg after she got her savings back up? I know her car brakes kept giving her trouble."

Mrs. Pryor's bistre skin turns ashen. She wavers.

"Abilene died last year, dear," she says. "We sent you an invitation to the funeral."

You stare at the quivering woman in front of you. Your guts may as well be on the conveyor belt. Asking what happened is futile.

"Sorry," you say. "I didn't get it."

"We sent it to your apartment address."

"I wasn't living there for too long."

Mrs. Pryor's hands worry at her bonnet. No wedding band gleams her on fingers now. You doubt her ring would fit without adjustment anyway. She's dropped four sizes in everything.

"You're the last Woodward left in these parts. What have you been doing with your life, honey," she says, "now that everyone up and left?"

You can't tell if that's a question for you or herself.

"I don't know," you say.

The migraine medication clatters in its box. Mrs. Pryor flees without waiting for her change. You stumble to the break room to hold your head in your hands.

* * *

The Halved World

That Sunday night when you break down, you locate none of your fifteen cousin-siblings in the county phone book, or forwarding addresses, or married names, or anything, which is why you end up tearing one of your lookalike's hands free from the zip-ties and crawling beneath its disgustingly pliable arm, baked and bawling.

"I'm sorry," you tell it, dripping ash onto its collarbone with your joint while you sob into its cloying neck. "I've done you dirty. You're a shitty rotting vegetable, but you're all I've got. No one else is here. No one else wants to be here."

The lookalike's pupils twitch. Your heart clenches. You cry out.

It can't be alive. It wasn't on the vine long enough, your rational brain says. The rest of you screams, *It's alive enough to know what you're doing.* How else could it move?

You straddle the lookalike. The sap congealing on the milkweed muscle sticks to your knee. The graffiti you carved into its waist yesterday scratches you. The lengthened, decomposing umbilical wilts beneath your weight. A splash of water from the jar splatters the lookalike's thighs.

"Here."

You're blubbering as you tilt its jaw up. Saline drowns your vision. You nearly cough to death on your first drag before you puke spit onto the hardwood. You sniffle, finish gurgling, then wipe your face. Your vision is no better than before.

"I'll give you a treat," you say. "You're gonna be compost anyway. Sorry. Here, here."

You take a deep pull of the joint. The lookalike's mouth opens with a moist click when you jam your fingers into the sides and squeeze. You lean in. The clack of its teeth against yours startles you. Your exhale of weed smoke vanishes into the lookalike's throat. Instead of bouncing back, it flows into sinus chambers connected to somewhere.

You hear squirming.

With the sound of an overripe melon splitting, the back of the lookalike's head bursts open. It spills forth seeds, dreamsicle pulp, and the true movers in the lookalike's rotting shell: a sea of white, writhing worms.

When you're done screaming, you sweep the worms into a grocery bag. Tear out the hair that has gunk entwined in it. Tie the bag. Cover the lookalike with a tarp. Crawl into bed, sniffling, angrily alone.

You don't have the heart to drag that overgrown buffet out back tonight.

* * *

You're fiddling with your radio, tuning it to the country station you like, one foot on the bike pedal, when you see her coming up the sidewalk. Frankie Hartnell has bad highlights and a blown-out butterfly tattooed on her stomach now, but she's the same glorious bitch she was in high school.

"Don't get off your bike." Frankie guards her growing belly with a palm. Her two broken french tips gleam against the butterfly's wings.

"Frankie," you say, weak. "Jesus Christ. It's been forever. What's going on?"

Frankie's exhale misses several stairs on its way down to you. Her gummy vitamins, batteries, and kitschy bibs rattle in her grocery bag.

"Can't you check a newspaper to get caught up?" she says. "Fuck. Stop calling me. My boytoy works the night shift. I've had to keep the phone off the hook so you don't wake him up."

"I want to hear from my best friend."

You feel as misshapen and inarticulate as your lookalike.

Frankie's frown overflows with pity. She fiddles with her clutch.

"I don't know how to tell you this," she says, "but being your only friend ain't something that makes me your best one. Not on my end. Please let this go, for your sake and mine."

"Everything's up and changed." You don't know why you're pleading, or what you're pleading for, but you want there to be some kind of truth living in all the space in your clothes and lungs. "I ain't heard shit from anyone. Abilene's dead. Did you know that Abilene was dead?"

"Abby and I hadn't talked for a year before she died," Frankie says. "I imagine there's a reason your own cousins aren't talking to you either."

"Look, I didn't hurt no one," you say. "That's not why I did time. But everyone treats me like a leper. Frankie, I can't keep paying bills or handling family business with the job I'm working. You've gotta know if another place will hire me."

"I am sorry, y'know," Frankie forges on, "but I'm barely staying afloat myself."

A singer croons about killing women in the gap that tears open between the two of you. The urge to swing builds in your fists, outstripped by the urge to cry. You can't swing at Frankie now. It wouldn't be a fair fight.

"Good luck." Frankie rubs her temple. "Honest."

"I don't want luck," you say. "I want *help*."

"Pray," Frankie suggests as she climbs into her death trap of an ancient jeep.

It sounds a lot like 'drown.'

* * *

Dusk falls into something darker as you bike towards your trailer. You're the sort of homesick that includes your body too, so you spent hours biking around downtown, hoping to find recognition here as you avoided your family plot. You found nothing. None of the whitewashed storefronts are as they were, none of the people the same. How has the world changed so much in two years? Whatever you've lost, there's no way to get it back.

You hunch over your grainy radio. Grass swats your legs, whispering. Charley Pride comes in and out of static, singing of snakes crawling at night. Castor and Pollux are above you with all the sneakers caught in telephone lines.

It takes a moment to realize the trailer door is a black, open rectangle.

It takes another to realize someone is in the driveway.

Gravel spins. Your bike stops. You stare at the gnarled, naked figure twelve feet in front of you. Their face is not in the light. You make out the pale square of muscle well enough. The zip-tie hanging from a leaking wrist. Bleeding graffiti. Here and there, a worm falls through the flashlight beam. You cannot tell who moves when the flashlight begins flickering.

As it gives out, you hear the crunch of feet on gravel. A horrible peace germinates within you. Freedom is coming. In a sense.

Sometimes, you imagine, the self wants to taste back.

LESS DEAD

When asked, Dad says, *Don't worry about Ximena—she's just a girl good at running away,* but you find a shoebox of condoms, calling cards, Selena CDs, baby name lists, and blush palettes squashed between a bed leg and a wall, the last of Ximena in her whirlwind-emptied room, which reminds you of Diva Fridays:

Come on, she'd say, *I'll teach you about eyeshadow,* before putting her heavy handed brushstrokes on your lids, which made you miss Marco—who lived in her room before he too fled—all cropped shirts, eyeliner, and laughter mixed with hair oil and truancy.

He had a box of condoms too.

The animals look like them, you tell Mom. She doesn't understand that squirrels are gnawing with baby teeth, raccoons developing pink palms, vultures singing raspy cumbia, your beagle watching you through Marco's eyes rimmed in black skin; she sees only laundry, lunch boxes, and outlines.

One Saturday, after you follow these animals into high weeds, burrs on your socks, Dad-tied pigtails on your head, you find the rotted lumps they're eating: skin and bear paw people-fingers and maggots plated on shattered bones. It smells like basement.

Your dad says it's just deer. Leave it alone.

Later, a woman calls you, asking if you've seen Ximena. She barely speaks English. You finger landline phone curls, safe and bored, before saying *No.*

No have money to call again, she says, *so please—*

Get more money then.

You hang up.

Many bad, fun runaways later, when police turn your boneyard into a poppy field of flags and shoot your animals for evidence, Mom weeps, vowing *I didn't know,* while you tell yourself that you lied to be good, to be a girl missed, knowing you lied for no reason at all.

sharp house

I'D HEARD THE RUMORS ABOUT WHAT HAPPENED TO those exploring the Sharps House: the mutilations; the flesh stripped from calf bone in shreds of moist tissue paper; the cheek wiped clean off skull to reveal scalded tongue; the decimations. The punctures. But until April, I never went inside. All of the flayings seemed like exaggerations of natural fractures that came from stupid, careless infractions. Any able youth could call themselves an explorer and get themselves hurt. I was certain that most victims grew drunk on both tall tales and the drink in hand before they broke into the Sharps House, always with something to prove, before landing themselves in a distant urban hospital.

When my friends and I broke in, our motivation was different.

Partially. We weren't unsober. We weren't out to investigate any phenomena. Our motivation, in hindsight, was cruel. We treated the Sharps House like an old, arthritic horse. We forced its mouth open to see its ringed teeth for no other reason than we could, then giggled at the fact we'd managed it without being bitten. The unity that cruelty brought comforted us. We refused to consider that our luck lasted as long as it did because the house and its resident were tired, meek, and uninterested in intentional brutality.

We knew just enough to be dangerous.

Just enough to get us past the gate and briar-choked driveway without being caught. Enough to force the front door. To kick aside tetanic debris with boots while we laughed at those before us who'd explored unarmored. Someone had tried cleaning. They'd swept ceramic figurine shards into loving piles, organized crockery, and set the moldy table. We sent their housekeeping to hell:

We hurled bottles against every stained surface, broke rot-fragiled furniture, smashed cobwebbed dishes, scattered silverware, ripped down hanging photos, stomped out what remained of the figurines, tore moth-eaten napkins, and spray-painted antiquities, laughing and howling all the while, a hurricane of joy. We defiled that dead home.

The Sharps House had long been destroyed by invaders. Still, the way it cradled its last possessions—its reputation, its vulnerable reality—made violence so, so satisfying. We relished outdoing the recognizable kudzu, hand, and weather scars.

What we didn't recognize were the scrapes.

They skinned the hardwood floor in loopy, unbroken trails that ate through the house; they splattered the walls in bleachy thorns. The trails and touches of some pacing dementia patient made of acid. Some spots near the windows were worn to near translucency. The moonlight that leaked through glass, grime, and boards struck these places like lantern light against an ear. The stench of a breakneck plummet to the basement wafted up through them. And where there wasn't moonlight, there was worse—sewing needles.

Since we lacked a way to satisfactorily hurt them, we let them be. But stray clumps of needles bristled from the scrapes on the walls and floor, silver lines tilting against dark, dark rot. They puzzled everyone. To me, they looked like luminous stems of fungi. A tiny, drowned portion of me thought, *They're beautiful.* I didn't dare say it. I stared at them even as my friends mocked me. Eventually, my friends' ribbing faded. The needles stayed. I saw their burning slants when I closed my eyes.

They were eyeless. This made them incapable of mending or creating anything. My friends called them nails. Yet I knew they were *needles*. This fact felt important. I said so aloud before I realized everyone had ventured deeper into the house. I was alone. Then I heard screaming and pounding footsteps in the basement.

The scraping.

All the scraping.

Figures burst from the basement stairwell. My friends. They were less people than a flock of panicked limbs and whites of eyes. Terror and scratches split faces I once knew into dripping, abstract pieces. Neither concern nor recognition lit them. My friends sprinted past me and ripped open the door. I cried out for them; they departed anyway.

The scraping sound pulsed closer. It crunched its way from basement stairwell to landing to sitting room. It was three hundred dried snake spines sticking and unsticking; it was mouthfuls of broken enamel meeting wood. It knitted me in place, even as my friends abandoned me. It overrode any sounds of retreat.

It was less harsh on the senses than its origin.

What resided in the Sharps House was not made of flesh. It was scribbles carved into the surface of existence. A blinding, shifting mass of needles that mimicked people-shape.

With every step it took, a layer of floor followed. Oak ripped like fiber. It cut my retinas to look at the thing; my ears bled to hear it. It broadcasted ruin. Immolation. Iron.

It turned towards me, as if it could see past itself, and parted its face. If I had seen a wet pocket of red, I could've bore it all. But there was no mouth—just a silver dent in silver hell, endless needles that rasped out a multisyllabic cadence—no hands—just mangled, shooting star imitations of them that raised pleadingly at me—and no body: just an infinity of needles, hunching, impossible.

When the rasping repeated a tenth time I screamed. I bolted. My foot crunched straight through a worn board. I plunged towards the abyss before a burning vice caught my wrist, yanked me up, and tossed me away. Fluid hosed me as I caught myself on the doorframe. I looked.

My wrist was obliterated.

An emptiness. A steaming void. Severed, shredded tubes against pinkish bone against shredded, dripping skin against geysers of blood; when my tendons pulled like little gossamer levers and pulleys, a broken needle rolled under one. It stuck. The agony was so enormous and sudden, I couldn't comprehend it. My whole body clenched.

I stared as the handful of me gushed out of the thing's grip, blendered by edges. It splattered onto the floor. Even my blood fled the needles. The thing knelt. It tried to grab a napkin. Decimated it. Tried again, again, until cotton wisps floated over the gore. In a wail of metal, the thing batted the wisps towards me. It cowered. It crawled in my spraying copper. It dipped its mitts into my slush while it rattled in rhythmic bursts. It started gathering a broken dish.

It did not chase me when I fled from it and the fall that had nearly killed me, wristless, friendless, its thousand-razor grip burnt into my phantom flesh, its horrible mantra clarifying in my mind:

sharp house

why was i made?
why can't i die?
i want to be gentle
i want to be kind.

Lithopedion

THey tell me, *Good ones behave.* I suck on the idea of goodness as I suck paste from my feeding tube. I stare at my cage walls. Outside of them is my everything: a field of algae and fringy strands of hydrilla. That's all there is. Algae, hydrilla, and harvesters. Sometimes, on strong currents, there's ash from the dead world, bitter and clingy and strange. But that doesn't last—the world before didn't either—so it doesn't matter.

There are always harvesters; there always will be. Trying gets me nothing, but if I try, I can tell them apart. I always recognize my harvester. She's with me more often than sunlight. She's small. She swims in scared little fish jerks. Every day, she lowers sensors into my cage, feeds me, and scrubs my shell.

This is a lifelong responsibility, a bigger, older harvester tells her. *You're an adult now.*

I know, my harvester promises. *I'm taking it seriously. I'm taking being an adult seriously.* She sticks to the older harvester when he's there. She perches on the pier above and kicks her feet when he's not. She sits on my cage to rest her feet on top of me and says *I'm in love, Shelly. Kill me.* Her toes scrunch against my flat womb skins. The others curl into the wave of my shell.

My harvester looks over her shoulders. She does it three times, as if there's anyone around in the maze of empty docks right now, or as if anything but harvesters lives on land. She leans over me.

Do you know what being in love is like? she says. *You're a girl too. You must.*

If that's the sensation of being handled, then I do.

***

They seed my wombs with beads first. Little balls made of wood, or scale lumps, or unfamiliar shell-spirals pieces. The shining baby-cysts I make from those are wrong. They pop out tiny and lumpy, their wrists fused to their necks and their limbs fused to each other. They don't even have faces. Some of them are dull. Every time I make one, the harvesters slide their fingers inside my sacs. They stretch them. *Not ready,* they say; *not yet.*

Why are you doing that? my harvester says.

We're getting the wombs ready for real pearls. The older harvester spreads his fingers inside one of my wombs. It itches. My harvester leans over as the older one starts pointing at lines inside me. *You see this? The arteries in her mantle haven't broadened yet. Without that blood flow, we can't insert a high quality nucleus. She'll spit it out. Or worse: waste it on a bad pearl.*

She looks too small to make pearls.

She isn't. Not really. In their excuse for a society, it would take twenty or thirty more years for her to be pearl-bearing, if she bore pearls at all. But with the right treatment, she can make them now.

Lithopedion

My harvester giggles. *We're the same age. Can you imagine me getting kidney stones, or having babies?*

The older harvester starts curling his fingers inside me.

You've grown up a lot, he says.

My harvester turns red. When we're alone again, she shoves her flashlight into my eye arcs. Its white overwhelms me. She leaves the flashlight there while she jams paste into my feeding tube. She turns the hose on so fast that my food blasts into me. I almost choke. I barely get to filter it.

Later, my harvester says sorry. Maybe that's supposed to mean something. To me it's like waves saying sorry for hitting the dock.

* * *

I don't remember much. All I do is be. Still, some memories sit inside me like baby-cysts the harvesters haven't taken away. I recall Bigger Me holding me against her white belly and gills with her shell-spirals closed around me. She had pairs of long, white legs that folded against her body in the closed shell. I had them too, even with rubber bands under my knees making mine crinkle and waste. Bigger Me talked. I didn't understand her.

After wombs pimpled my body the harvesters took me from her. They tied me to a beam away from her and injected juice into the soft back between my shell hinges. If I remember pain, it was when that needle-tip shoved into my spine, or when they cut me open to thread cables around my spine. But my body liked that because it started gushing stick-forever paste. Now, even if I didn't have the cables through me, I wouldn't roll off the beam. When my sick legs fell off, I didn't feel anything.

My harvester's changes are different. They occur on their own. The flesh on her chest begins swelling. Itsy-bitsy womb sacs full of fluid cover her cheeks. Every time I glimpse my harvester without her respirator there are more of them. Sometimes, during a dive, she leaks blood. She begins asking if I can talk.

The savage ones can, she says. *Why not you?*

I'm changing too. My shell-spirals begin flushing red and rainbow. They thicken. A deep current of badness starts opening in my veins. Whenever little blue-touched crabs walk up my cage I blow bubbles at them until they fall off. I begin wishing all my arms would work besides twitching. Whenever invisible legs appear under my knees, pinching, flexing, I try kicking. For the first time, opening for harvesters feels bad in my brain, not just my body. Why should I do it? I start looking for the dead world's oil dust. Whenever I suck it into my filters I hold its taste there a long time.

During low tide my harvester puts her arms around me and touches me. Sometimes she touches one of my faces then touches her face. She looks around to make sure the cages around us are empty before she does.

You're melted, compared to the wild ones, she says, *or diagrams of your grandma. You're ugly. Poor Shelly. We'll get through this. You're my friend.*

Friend. Mother. Grandmother. What do those words mean?

* * *

I dream of other Mes shackled to beams, gnarled with baby-cysts, sucking on paste and sedatives and not remembering anything, just filtering moments and harvester memories. I need to dream of them. They're in cages somewhere else in the dock maze but I can't and won't ever be with them.

Why can't my oystoid talk to the others? Wouldn't it be

better for her to have friends? Or maybe even, um, well, a boyfriend?

The other harvesters laugh.

Are you stupid? one says.

She doesn't ask again.

* * *

The water turns cold, perfect for shell growing—perfect for clouds of big-eye silver finger fishes to squirt eggs at each other—before the harvesters start seeding me with grandmother nuclei. My wombs cling to those. They know those nuclei are intruders. They also recognize them. They start building lacquer skeletons around them.

You're doing so wonderful, the harvesters coo, squeezing the hard growths along my limbs. Their words and fingers mean little to me. They are just bubbly rattles through respirators and fish-bright flashes of touch. I lay on my steel beam and wait for the fingers and extractor loops to get out of me.

This one only needs three more months! my harvester says. She shows her coworker the fistful of cyst on my collar. The eyes rimming my ribs, the ones that still work, can see a glittery skull poking from the womb sac.

Be careful, another harvester says, *or you'll damage it.*

He means the baby-cyst.

* * *

The moon makes me restless. When it's full, close, and tugging, its light gets through the dead world dust. It makes me dream. In my dreams I'm see-through and squishy. I hide beneath Bigger Me's arms. Her pulse drums me. I understand her words, but not what she means. *We're the good ones,* she insists. *If we behave, they won't hurt us. We made our pact because we're smart. We'll survive.* She pets the rubber bands disappearing into my legs. Every time I wriggle, I bump against her seeded wombs. The eyes bunched on my elbows let me look into one and its baby-cyst pushing at the entrance has my faces without meat.

My dream ends in a burst of screams, quakes, and splashes. Everything is shaking: the sand, the hydrilla, my beam, me. The moonlight breaks. Blood washes into my filters. It isn't mine. A black, broken rip thrashes through the moonlight water. I don't recognize it until my spine stops trying to shake in half. It's the older harvester. He's swim-flailing around, puffing out blood.

A long knife made of rock hangs out of his ribs. It has a tail of broken wood. As other harvesters yank the older harvester onto the dock it falls out of him. Its tail of mermaid purse and shell beads tickles me as it tumbles to the bottom. It rolls under my stubs. Since I don't have anything else to hide, I hide it: I nudge it beneath me with my stubs, then drape my gummy limbs and lower siphons over it.

The thought of having a warm baby to hide stabs me.

My harvester doesn't feed me at sunbirth. She doesn't feed me at high sun either. The currents are dense with vibrations. The harvesters scramble over the net of docks all day. Torch flames and hammer rings echo above the waves at low tide. My harvester finally comes at sundeath. Her hair is melted and stuck in her wetsuit zipper. Her eyes are red. She shakes every time she shoves paste into my feeding tube. At the end of feeding she drops onto the dock. She cries so loud I don't know if she's breathing.

This isn't fair, she says. *It's not right. This shouldn't happen anymore. The war is over. We won.*

I almost give her the knife. I could, if I blew enough bubbles over it. She would come look. That would be good. All the swelling baby-cysts in my wombs ache.

Lithopedion

An oil-dark, bitter thought opens in me: I don't want to be good. I don't want to give her anything at all.

One sunbirth, while I am trying to be dead so I am not here, the older harvester limps onto the dock. He's in robes that flow around his stitched-up ribs. All the shelling lining on his ears and belt jingles. My harvester grabs all over him. She cries, telling him, *I'm so glad you're healed. I was so scared.* This goes on forever. The noise becomes an itchy, horrible nucleus under all of my skin. She quiets when the older harvester gives her a ring. It has a pearl at its center: a chunk from my last baby.

My harvester gasps. She begins crying. She puts the ring on. They wrestle on the dock for a while before the older harvester peels his pants open. Then he yanks my harvester's wetsuit down too. Its folded shape chains her shins together. The older harvester grows a siphon. He wiggles it inside my harvester. He thrusts it. He grabs my harvester's hand and forces her ring into her face. *Look,* he says. *You're mine.*

Yes, yes, my harvester cries. They clutch each other until the older harvester pulls away. Mucus leaks out of my harvester and between the dock boards. The older harvester zips his suit up.

Clean up, sweetheart, he says, *before someone sees you.*

My harvester sniffles before she laughs. It echoes off the surface. *Okay.*

The blade kicked under me didn't cut my meat, but before I hid it beneath sand and shell, it cut me. It cut my mind. It let badness in.

Why should I eat? There's a whole world outside of my cage. Maybe it's not dead. There wouldn't be soggy, pointed dead leaves from elsewhere stuck against my cage if it was dead. Why can't I taste that world instead? Even if it's dead, why can't I be with other Mes? If I scrunch my siphon, I can spit out the feeding tube. I glow inside when my mealpaste spills onto my shell instead of into my filters. Until my harvester has to stick it back in every feeding, until that's all I know, I start closing my shell and sucking my siphon in so she can't.

The weight of all my seeded wombs shoved together makes a pressure so heavy that it almost explodes me in half. Hearing my harvester beg me to be nice while she fails to pry my shell open convinces me to stay shut. Badness satisfies me more than any paste. Choosing when harvesters touch me is worth any pressure, even if they always win.

Will they always?

My harvester starts jamming spreaders in my shell to keep it open. I spit them out. Once, I crunch one in half. I'm wild-lonely. I won't take this anymore. I want to tear my spine out and leave it on the beam. I want to leave. When I'm not screaming, my body hums. It wants to spray soft eggs into the world. It wants someone else to spray them with life. It wants other Mes, from inside me and outside me. If I had to eat my own stomach to get that I would.

My harvester cries every time she's around me. *Be good, Shelly,* she pleads. *I know you hate it here, but be good.* She's slower and throws up now. She inches her hand towards the older harvester's hand, as if she can sneak up on it. When she brushes his fingers he crosses his arms. He's looking at me. My harvester withers.

The older harvester says, *She's maturing. That's all. Rebellion is normal.*

No. She's caged. She's miserable. She's losing her mind. I'd lose mine too. Could you imagine living in a prison your whole life?

Oh, don't project on her. She's in heat. This is why we keep them separate from the males. He smiles. *Maybe sticking a different kind of tube in her would calm her down.*

My harvester is trying to reach for his hand again when he says that. It changes her. She shoves him so hard she almost hurls both of them off the dock. *Leave!* she screams. *Fucking leave! I can't stand you!* She throws fistfuls of paste at him, yelling, until he stops arguing. He leaves. Then my harvester flops belly-down on the dock, wincing. I stay open to watch her. She traces my faces with her fingertips. She cries.

They want us and use us, she says, *but they don't understand us.*

Who's 'us'?

* * *

Forgetting Bigger Me's words has consequences.

On the sundeath I learn this, I'm upside-down. Good looks bad; bad looks good. My harvester is reaching inside me to check my wombs. A rush shoots through me. Every tool and gloved finger that's ever been in me is in me again; every time my harvester has chosen to let the older harvester in her is pressing on every thread of me.

My harvester didn't stick a spreader between my shells. I shut on her arm. It crunches. Bubbles spray out of my harvester's respirator. She thrashes. *I choose!* I yell at her. *I choose!* I choose to free her, too. She floats up more than swims. Someone pulls her onto the dock.

At low tide, other harvesters wade to me. They bring thick cutters with long legs. They cut my shell off. It crunches off in giant, flaky plates. Every time the cutters close, their crunch echoes all the way into my middle. They leave just enough shell behind to keep my insides cupped together. Otherwise I'd sag onto the mud. The shock of my nakedness always against the currents slaps my gills so hard that I almost stop breathing. This feeling is too huge.

The harvesters give me shots, massage me, and sew the feeding tube into my siphon. They make me live. My harvester cries on the pier above me under moon and sun. While her arm is purple and crooked, she's not allowed to dive around me. She keeps saying *I'm sorry.*

This continues until the older harvester begins sitting with her. He holds her. *You did the right thing. They don't feel pain,* he reassures her. *They're not sentient anymore.* At the end of every talk, he pins my harvester's head onto the dock and shoves his siphon inside her. After enough repetitions, my harvester stops disagreeing. After they seed me with enough polished, red-and-rainbow nuclei, I stop caring.

When I get married, I'll live in a house on the cliffs. That way, I can see beautiful sunsets on the bay, but not ever be attacked. I'll have my own bed. I'll have three children. My husband will love them, and me. I'll get him to dig a saltwater pond for you in the yard. You'll get to see all the flowers and tomatoes that your people's shells help grow. You'll get to eat them, and not just the horrible oil you keep away from them. We'll be best friends. No more cage. No more guilt. You'll never have to make pearls again, and I'll finally be free. I'll have made up for everything I've done.

Can you imagine it, Shelly? The future will be perfect.

I begin yelling into the bay so my mind doesn't crush me.

Lithopedion

Every day, my scent-calling spills into the saltwater, where it washes far away. It's strange to know that part of me escapes. I've never known movement that includes me. Sometimes, when currents blast me with pebbles, I try choking on them. The harvesters set up filters to keep them away. I'm already attached to concrete and steel, but they dig out the tan, floaty mud around me and put in concrete there too. They also wrap chains around my wrists, drill holes in what's left of my shell, screw hooks into the holes, then stick my wrist chains on the hooks. My arms are sedative-floppier than hydrilla and I've never used them but maybe they're afraid I will. If I could use them, I would shovel pebbles into my gills until I died.

I sleep while awake too much to count the baby-cysts they take out of me. I lay on the knife. I rock what's left of my shell every night and wriggle the knife further beneath me. Everything disappears into black spots whenever my meat loosens around the cables but I don't care. It lets me move. Grain by grain, the stick-forever paste crumbles. Grain by grain, the knife moves. It's the one part they don't know. It's the one part they didn't take. I need it.

My harvester rants about a future that doesn't come. *I wish you could get engaged, Shelly,* she tells me. *Actually, I don't. It's awful. Pretending that there's nothing between us is torture. At least the wedding is soon. He said it's soon.*

Soon, the bay cools. Soon, a trickle of warmth breaks its cool.

If there was a world before *soon* always fell from my harvester's mouth, I don't remember it.

* * *

When the baby-cyst on my neck gets so big that it's crushing my collar, they thread a ventilator brush into my gills to keep me from suffocating. Lights shine in my eyes; tools and hands probe my sac. I'm floating out of my body. They must've increased the sedative. They do that a lot after they trimmed my shell.

Breathe, the older harvester urges. My harvester's gloves fumble around my womb sac. She's trying to fit an extractor over the fattest part. I realize that it's latching into me and cutting me—and has been—because of the metal catching my vision edges and the mirage clouds flowing out of me. Blood. The harvester's arm keeps hitting one of the spreader-bars that holds my trimmed shell open. The harvesters around her buzz like stirred hydrilla leaves.

Finally, my harvester gets her extractor over the womb sac. She cinches it around the base. She pulls. Under bubble-blurred lights, under glove grip, a pearl baby bursts out of me. If it was ever alive, it's been dead for a long time; it's hard and curled. Its stone nosebones snag my mantle on their way out.

The harvesters wipe it off. They put it in a bag and feel it. *Gorgeous,* the older harvester says, *triple A grade, maybe quadruple A.* My harvester is shaking. Behind her respirator, she's smiling. My agreement catches on ventilator brush ridges. My mindwaves are wobbly. I can't pay attention to the harvesters.

They take my baby-cyst away. Another harvester, one with tongs, opens a murky tube. They take a polished ball of bone from it. The tube's fluid stains the water. *Grandmother nucleus,* she says, like I have a grandmother. A different harvester scribbles that onto a notebook. As she does, the first harvester opens my deflated womb sac with a speculum. Its paddles widen the rip my baby's skullface made. She pushes the bone ball in. There's tight, tight pressure as it seeds. Is this pain too? I wonder that every time. They rub the edges of my sac with cleaning gel and clamp it shut. The blood clouds tighten into a leak.

Ridge by ridge, the ventilator brush slithers out of my gill-throat. It pops free in a bloom of pressure and mucus. For a second, it's something else born from me. Then, in another flutter, it's gone. The two harvesters left measure my other womb sacs. They rattle off collection timeline dates; they remind each other which womb has grandmother or mother nuclei in it. Finally, they leave. Then I am alone again.

* * *

One sundeath, my harvester drops the bucket of mealpaste she's carrying out to me. She moans. She falls onto the dock. She rips her pants off and pushes out a baby. It arrives in its own miniature bay. It's warm and has a face. Other harvesters rush to her. They carry her and the baby away. She gets to hold it as they do. There's so much screaming on the shore that it washes out to me. After that, my harvester isn't mine. From then on, the older harvester is. He touches me hard and short. Sometimes, he carries the baby out to look at me. By the time I get the knife squeezed halfway between my back and the beam I'm tied to, the baby walks. When I get the knife into the soft spot between my back and the beam, it talks. It's a gurgly, clumsy little harvester.

I lean hard on the knife when it looks at me.

At the hottest, brightest water time, a harvester I don't recognize approaches me. Wrinkles net her cheeks. Her belly sticks out from her robe. She's seeded. I don't recognize my old harvester until she strokes the surface with a pearl-ringed finger.

Hey, Shelly, she says.

She tells me that she married the older harvester. She tells me about her child, how happy she is, and how excited she is about the war really ending. I learn a new word: daughter. Now that my harvester is grown up, she knows that I'm spoiled. *It was silly to dream that you'd live in my yard,* she says. *That would be impossible. Especially with the shortage. I'm sorry. You forgive me, right?* She smiles. *I knew you would. You're my girl.*

The harvester's smile fades with the sun. She holds her belly while the dock spotlights flash on.

Life never works out the way you want it to, she says.

* * *

I dream of harvesters stroking the polished pieces of my baby-cyst inset in their rings. *How lucky we are,* they sing, their little thems dancing around them. They eat sweet, fresh pastes straight from a living world. *How beautiful everything is!*

I wake to moon and movement. There is a shape watching me. It stands behind the hydrilla, twisty and full of moon. Is it a harvester tangled in weeds? No. It pushes the hydrilla away from my cage. Its arms reach from between the long teeth of its open shell. They're spiraled in glittery spikes. Reed robes drape over it except for where its eyes wavecrest on its chest. Beads dangle around its legs. Its faces all stare at me. They are whirlpools of pretty mantle petals pretending to be harvester faces.

The shape has a stone knife. Its long wooden tail isn't broken. This thing must be another me. Except how can it be? There's not a single womb with baby-cysts on it.

Bubbles burst out of its siphons. It starts churning. It makes sounds I don't understand.

I have your knife, I tell it. *Come get it. Let me touch you. Let me out.*

Its sounds get louder and choppier. It rips its hands off the cage.

No. Let me out!

I try waving my limbs. They ripple a little. They make the feeding tube sewed into my siphon drift into my faces and catch on my seeded wombs. The other me stumble-swims backwards. Its noises crash together. A sour smell pours from it: fear. Fear, and fear, and fear. It's screaming.

It runs away.

* * *

This is the last time I'll be bad.

Not because I want to be good, but because being bad is hard. It opens me with speculums that smell like a different world then lets harvesters keep seeding me. It lets my cage smash me. It tells me what's gone. It shoves emptiness into me through its feeding tube. Badness grew inside me until it was a baby-cyst bigger than the moon that was splitting me open, then never left. It showed me that I know pain.

Being good is easy. It's giving up. Giving up lets me live without looking at pain. Goodness makes my mind small, but my cage is small too. I have to fit in it.

This last time that I'm bad, I let my mind break the cage. There's sedative and harvester fingers in me. I break from them. I dream that I'm out. I dream of choosing: choosing when to eat, choosing no baby-cysts, choosing to remember. The moon is there. She touches my long, curly shell while I burrow into silt to sleep. I like it.

I dream that my old harvester gives birth to a stone baby-cyst. I more than dream it. I make it real. If I can create baby-cysts inside me, why can't I create them inside someone else? I focus on that idea until I shake. I make a tiny, white hot sun of will; I imagine it burning into my harvester. Into every seeded harvester. Veins pop in my mantle. Some rip under a speculum's paddles. My stubs kick. My back bulges out of my shell hinge. It wraps the knife. It screams; I scream: *I choose!* I rock.

My back bursts.

Then, there's pain. Then, the knife lives inside. Its edges

rake the cables running around my spine. It tears me. The harvesters shriek. All of me begins leaking into the bay. I know, then, that my dream is becoming.

My harvester's womb-wrapped baby will be gray. Its skull will be melted into its excuses for arms. It will be curled, pitted, and become heavier every day. It will be rougher than broken shell. *Come out dead,* I urge it, *or stay in her forever. Make her understand.* My baby-cysts ache under my skin. They cry.

The harvesters are arguing in sharp bubble sprays and putting lots of clamps on the wrong places. They check the pulses on my wrists over and over. *How? Why? Hurry!* they repeat, as if that will fix me. It's funny. My mirage springs of blood keep flowing out. Either I'll die, or I'll finally birth something good.

Do they know what a curse is? I do.

EGREGORE

for all drunk girls in the bathroom.

«I SAID NO. I'M SCARED.»

It's the third time you've asked this clubber to repeat herself. A speaker is blasting behind you, grainy, blown-out, overwhelming in its sonic output—it's not just your ear drums, the ancient floor is vibrating too—and even by the bar, all is lit by failing pink strobe lights.

Pulsing streaks of skin hover where the clubber's face should be. A glitching collection of maybe-features and maybe-flesh broken by glimmers of metal. Above her, a lopsided fan rattles; behind her, the club seethes, a sea of broken light and grinding, amorphous bodies. Grimy mirrors armor every wall, making the crowd thirty-fold.

«Okay,» you say.

Your miniskirt and halter top are sheets dripping off your body, textile made liquid heat. Your thighs stick to the broken chair beneath them. The cocktail you paid too much for is clammy in your hand. The crisped vape coil stench won't leave. The clubber won't either.

«To the dance,» the clubber says. «I said no when she asked.»

«Who?»

«The woman between women space.»

She must be new. She has no eyebrows. Her eyeliner wings are vast, thick wedges of tar. In the strobes, they're voids. If you hook your fingers into her temple holes and pull, you could peel away her face in strips. You imagine her countenance would crumple into your fist like a condom's warm latex.

«Hun,» you say, «that's a lesbian.»

«That's me. I'm scared,» she says.

«Okay.»

All the strobing shards of skin around where her voice emerges scrunch in, forming a strange carnation of features. She gurgles in the split lull between songs. Oh. She's crying. The clubber seizes your elbows with crushing, spit-wet hands.

«I'm freaking.» Her shaking rattles the cocktail out of your cup. It splatters your lap. «I'm really freaking.»

You grab one of her wrists. «Let's go to the bathroom.»

You don't hear what she says next. You absorb syllables framed by a warped, flashing elastic of lip. Maybe the bathroom is quieter. Or cooler. These factors matter to people. You drag the clubber away from the speaker, across shores of gyrating bodysea, and into a bathroom made of brick and collapsing stalls. They're more graffiti than mauve paint or wood.

A group of girlies is clustered around two sinks and their mirrors. They're a chattering cluster of stiletto nails, coquette sunglasses, and utterly owned bodies. They writhe over each other to fix their lip gloss in the mirrors. You tow the clubber to a sink nearby. In the bathroom's steady glow, she gains a face. It's ashen. Swollen. She's young. Bloody opals hover in the crooked, moist corners of her mouth.

«What's her problem?» A girlie points at the clubber. Her pigtails crawl over her shoulders and into her glittery cleavage in so many reaching tendrils.

«Negative space,» you say.

A girlie laughs. «That's all of us.»

You rinse your cup, then plug the sink with paper towels and flood it with cold water. The clubber's pupils are so enormous they're sliding out of her. She slumps against the mirror. Although it's quieter, two speakers are audible from inside the bathroom. Both play the same song, with one a few seconds ahead of the other. Everything is ripply.

«Does she want a pick-me-up?» A girlie looks up from hooking the plum curve of her thong on a glittering, palm-length talon. Hearts and stars float in its quick.

The clubber's pupils shiver. Her dahlia piercings shift back and forth. You hear the grinding of teeth against piercing posts alongside the squelching tear of unhealed cheeks. You scoop water from the sink in your cup, wetting your fishnets, and hurl it into her eyes. Behind her, twin girlies draw ice picks from their ribbon-cinched leg warmers. Other girlies remove compacts and flip phones from their purses.

«Was a man it?» A girlie sets her bedazzled cane aside and wipes an ice pick on her skirt. It's a flannel ruffle that covers none of her. «I'll suck his skin off. Just give me the word, babe. I'll erase him.»

The clubber shakes her drenched head. You hurl another cup of water at her. She coughs. «It was the woman between women space.»

A girlie slides the ice pick beneath her sunglasses. It tips them up. You glimpse a deep bruise.

«She's gorg,» a girlie says.

«If you look,» the clubber says, «between people and mirrors—»

A spluttering, electronic beat floods the bathroom. It overwrites the sound of the running sink.

«ARMS, BODY, LEGS, FLESH, SKIN, BONE, SINEW» the speakers chant. «ARMS, BODY, LEGS, FLESH, SKIN, BONE, SINEW.»

All of the girlies scream.

«Yes!» they howl. «Yes!»

«—magic eye puzzle, the angle has to be—»

The clubber gestures while skirt girlie, dancing, reaches behind her sunglasses. She pinches her lashes between thumb and index finger. She pulls her eyelid up. She slides the ice pick beneath her glasses and over the top of her eyeball.

«—confusing because a lot's happened! I'm—»

Skirt girlie's reflection lip syncs as she angles the ice pick upward. She aims the flat side of her compact at it. A cascade of shooting star charms hang at the dull end of the pick. They jingle. Maroon cakes their tassels.

«—been alone until tonight, you're all—»

The music explodes out of both speakers. Skirt girlie drives the ice pick in with one clipped blow after another. She wiggles it back and forth, all her friends singing and dancing with her.

«—Nebraska so after my crush raped me I couldn't—»

One girlie plucks the shining ice pick from skirt girlie's socket as if it's a rose stem, a beam of light, and slides it under her own eyelid. They're experts: they grind on each other, skirt to skirt, breast to shimmying breast, synchronized to one beat or another. The pounding of compacts or flip phones on ice picks melds into the equally metallic music.

The song ends in one speaker before it ends in the other.

«What a banger,» a girlie says.

The clubber's melting liner contours her cheekbones in

black downpour curtains. She's skeletal. Long ago, you were liner-cry gaunt too.

«Feeling better?» you say.

«Sort of.» She wrings her fingers.

«Okay.»

You move to leave. The clubber clings to you.

«Wait!» she says. «Is the woman between women still out there?»

«Girl. She's a regular. An aggregation. She wants to dance, right?» A girlie looks at her from beneath fanning lashes. «So dance. Duh.»

The clubber's throat bobs.

«You need a pick-me-up,» a girlie says.

The clubber looks at her corded waist, complete with floating clover belly piercing, and says, «Sure. Sure.»

The girlies usher the clubber into their center. They crowd around her in a miasma of perfume and cunt. When her eyelid keeps shivering and shutting, one girlie pulls it open. An ice pick glows in another girlie's fist. You check your phone. Since you don't have a plan it never has new messages. You watch it die during the hammering and brain-stirring.

When it's over, you and the clubber wander back onto the dance floor. The music is a mixture of moaning and women screaming over a club beat that shakes grime out of every crevice in the decaying building. You prepare to groove. The clubber sways nearby, rubbery, relaxed. Bruised splotches float in her not-face now.

For the final time, the clubber stumbles into your orbit.

«Dance with me?» she pleads. «Until she shows?»

Though you want to reject her, the uncertainty in her voice—childish and untailored—verges on anxiety. It implies personhood. You were once a person too. It takes such little time before these raw, ruffled edges of being are wiped away. How many crucial moments have you lost to becoming?

«Okay,» you say.

You dance.

Song by song, strobestep by strobestep, you and the clubber wriggle your way into the middle of the dance floor. The view is different from the center. Instead of watching bodycurrents splash onto the dance floor's extremities before ebbing back, you're at the boiling apex. Slivers of corset, flinging hair, flexing muscle, and maybe-people crash together around you, all wet, twining, sometimes brushing you, sometimes pirouetting around you. The heat-reek throbs with the lights. It's somehow calmer here than on the outskirts. After several rounds, the clubber doesn't seem to know where she is. Your consciousness begins unsticking from your body.

In the endless labyrinth of reflections, between a flickering crossroads of elbows and knees, a shape manifests. It vanishes a millisecond after you register it. You're uncertain you parsed anything until, several steps and a head tilt later, you register it again: a shape. Electric wire. A moment. Sweat streams past your brows. It burns. You dance through the next song with your gaze on the floor. The clubber's sticky, bruised form stays against yours. She's oblivious.

A few songs later, when the music turns to sex toy plastic vocals and car crash sounds, music meant for girls that fuck for sport, you look behind the clubber again. It's easier to navigate the kaleidoscope this time. You let your vision slide between mirrors and mirrored, thrashing thighs and backs, and there it is, distant and prickly: the shape.

The figure.

The figure isn't an object. It's a presence between them. An outlined void. At the right angle, negative space clicks into an implication. Face or vase? When you solve the cipher, when you register her in full, pressure blooms in your skull. It bounces with the beat of sound and light. It throbs at the juncture of oncoming migraine or ice-pick-wiggle in frontal lobe or orgasm. The figure's outline intensifies into a glowing white grain.

She must be coming closer, because she's getting bigger.

You dance closer to the clubber. By the time atoms buzz around you, your jaw is almost slotted into the clubber's collar, your hips almost in her skirt. Her breath smells of mint and her maybe-skin smells of cheap stainless steel. You suspect she never had a face. If you took her maybe-mouth with yours you could chew her tongue and taste the bubble gum texture of all the bad schools and oil field trailers you lost your personhood in.

You doubt the clubber feels.

The figure is coming, inch by inch, girlie by girlie. You perceive her crawling between parted calves and squeezing between flirting pelvises. She grinds in ways the rest of you can't. Isn't the space between women more delectable, more violent, than their touch? The clubber is screaming at the ceiling or singing along. Who knows. You grab her shoulders.

«Look,» you say.

In the reflected cauldron of dancers, in their shadows, hovers an extended hand. An offer. The clubber grows still. If she has an expression it's lost to you. Her features are blurry commas pitting sludge. Her whole figure goes rigid. She's an unbreathing animal becoming stiff in a useless lap; a hole contracting around an intruder. For a fraction of time, you know her.

She exhales.

The clubber steps into the space between women. Her waist swivels. She dances into her new partner's dark matter arms. Then, she's gone. A dissolved patch of particles. A grainy burst in the dark. Pressure lifts from your temple. There's only pink lights, a lull between remixes, and the club. Someone's hoop earring crunches under your heel. A drunk, wheeling doll next to you is crying on her friend, her maybe-face smeared against breast.

«You're so beautiful,» she's saying. «You're so, so beautiful so.»

The next song begins, pulsing and unbearable and aloof.

You greet it with open arms.

Poolhorse

THEY CONDEMNED THE REC CENTER AFTER HER stepbrother Tyrese disappeared, but Brooklyn—now almost thirteen—sneaks in anyway. As she pushes on the faded pool room doors, she tells herself: "Maybe it's dry. Maybe there's nothing." Hopefully there's nothing. She doesn't want to keep this promise to her stepdad.

But no. The indoor pool is there. It stretches before Brooklyn in a sickly, aqua rectangle. It's full. The roof has collapsed, so a sunset-filled hole looms above the pool, complete with a moldy, dangling tongue of ceiling panels. Dead leaves rim the water until three feet out. The diving board is broken, the ladders lopsided and sinking, the depth markers faded off. All is still; all is deep.

Brooklyn can't go closer. She paces around broken sun loungers. Her throat is tight; her breathing hard. Every time she sniffles, it echoes in the ceiling mouth, which makes her anxious. Her fingers are tingling. Chlorine wedges itself under her gums. She's afraid if she throws up, it won't come out.

Finally, Brooklyn breaks out of her orbit around the chairs. She kneels at the poolside barefoot, sick with herself, rolling up her capris. This is what promises mean. This is what keeping them takes. When her foot taps the moist cake of decay on the pool and it doesn't give, Brooklyn gags. After some kicking, her feet break through. She sits at the deep end, bodywarm water stagnating around her calves. She waits.

She doesn't wait long.

It surfaces slowly. Its diamond nostrils show first. Then bulging, frog-pupiled eyes. Pointed ears. Its mane congeals on the surface like half-dried blood. It's all starved gaps between bone, rubbery skin, and oily horse stench. Butterfly clips, tiny press-on nails, hair ties, braces wires, pacifiers, and baby doll parts clutter its hair. Brooklyn trembles when it looks at her.

You're back, Poolhorse says.

When it speaks, its face-lid peels open up to its ears, flashing a spiral of teeth.

"Yeah," Brooklyn says. Then, remembering what saved her last time, she says: "You're still a pretty horse."

Poolhorse laughs. It sounds like a hurt baby screaming into pipes. A sparkly hair band and thread of scalp dangle from its teeth. Brooklyn feels nine again.

You won our little race. Bubbles blow out of Poolhorse's nose. Its barbed tongue worms out of its mouth, wiping its chin. Brooklyn feels it tasting her skin oils. *No one comes back after they win. And almost no one wins.*

"I didn't win because I was a good swimmer," Brooklyn says. "I won because I was faster than Tyrese."

That's all that matters.

"Poolhorse, I need what's left of him." Brooklyn's swallowed tears burn her nose. "A bone. Anything."

Why?

"Because I promised our dad I'd find him."

Poolhorse blinks its translucent eyelids. *I'll give him to you. If you play another game.*

"No games! I just want the missing poster to be gone! You don't need him."

Another game, Poolhorse repeats.

It's unfair that if she starts crying she'll never stop; it's unfair that her stepdad cries every day; it's unfair that Poolhorse is real just to kids; it's unfair that her stepdad thinks she's at a sleepover. That he might put her on a missing poster too. But everything is unfair.

"What game?" Brooklyn says.

Poolhorse drifts up to her paralyzed knees. It opens into a kaleidoscope of teeth.

Go fish, it says.

Poolhorse plays by rules written in toddler sidewalk chalk. Brooklyn is getting too old to read them. If she flees now, she might never get to try again. She remembers Poolhorse cornering them. The cold lightning terror that struck her. She remembers how she looked at slow, afraid Tyrese and accepted the race. Maybe her stepdad wouldn't say 'I love you' every night if he knew that. That scares her more than anything.

Brooklyn's fast breathing beats inside her ears. Sweat beads under her training bra. Her hand hovers above the pool, hemming, hawing. Poolhorse's stench clogs her nose. Tyrese's face floats in her mind. *I don't want to go like you,* Brooklyn tells him. *Sorry.* Shame sets in. Relief.

She's about to withdraw when Poolhorse's long neck twitches. Its teeth mandala clacks. Dead leaves crumple against Brooklyn's exposed calves. Hot, rotten breath mists her. Poolhorse is close. And impatient. She's been stupid. It doesn't matter if she loves her family enough or not. If Brooklyn is a bad sport, she'll immediately lose. There's only one way to maybe, maybe win. She licks her lips.

She reaches in.

Millimeter by millimeter, squirm by squirm, Brooklyn's hand works past rubbery lips, millions of canines, worm tongue, and stale screams. It passes elastic rings of throat. It digs into tissue. Poolhorse's fangs scrape her shoulder. Her armpit. Its drool floods her pores. Brooklyn is almost kissing Poolhorse's greasy forehead as she reaches into the infinite worst. She's squeezing its nose. Her muscles scream. If Poolhorse bites—

Please, she thinks, *please,* and below them rot ripples across heaven-bright pool water that used to be beautiful, broken just by Brooklyn's splashing legs and Poolhorse's downpour of drool. Then her fingers brush something slippery. Hard. Brooklyn seizes it. Poolhorse's throat tightens around her arm as she pulls it out. It's like dredging in molasses. It hurts. By the time Brooklyn yanks her fist out, black spots cover her vision.

Goodbye, pretty girl. Poolhorse sinks in a whirlpool of toys and hair.

Then it's gone.

Brooklyn scrambles out of the pool, scraping her palms and knees as she goes. When she can see, when she realizes that she's clutching a deflated water wing pierced by an arm bone, she wails. She drags herself onto a broken sun lounger and curls around her stepbrother's crumbs, hiccupping, bloody knees and tears smearing chair plastic. A dam shatters. She hemorrhages years of tears. It's over. They are going home.

And there is only Brooklyn, and grief, and golden hour, and—in the sun-pierced center of the pool—a stained water wing, drifting alone.

limerence

There's no seeing the moon under two meters of peat.

Soon, she tells herself, *soon,* but that's been the moss-cradled word in her mouth for over two thousand years. Her skin is leather, her organs shrunken, her bones dissolved—the bog, ever-faithful bed and jealous boyfriend, has taken those—but there's no cure for longing.

It's beautiful up there, she tells herself; *it must be.* Even with everyone she's ever known gone, there must still be storks, uncombed mounds of golden grass, and willow-laden laggs. Surely the bell heather still blooms. The village that plaited her hair put nightshade in her stomach to secure that bounty. It can't be gone.

There's another down there with her, in the belly of the bog, but he's more sphagnum than man. A mummy unspooled into the wool that makes them all; a weft end that ought to be tucked into a loom warp rather than seen. He's a half-meter below her. That may as well be a world. When she sinks, he does. They'll never touch. They'll never see each other. Since they died centuries apart, perhaps they were never meant to. They're parted and united by peat. All they can offer each other are words.

The unwoven man has a noose about his neck. The offering knows he must've been a criminal. Maybe a thief, murderer, or adulterer. She hasn't cared about such things since she died. Nor has he.

They are in love.

it is beau tiful, the criminal says. *I ca n feel it.*

I'd like to see the snow, she replies. *There must be snow. The peat is colder.*

is it?

Yes.

It's been centuries since the offering was high enough to feel the peat's warmth, or to even feel its changes. She can't sense these things when she speaks to the criminal. This is not lying—it's stretching truth to its finest fiber. Snow always comes; snow always goes. Flowers bloom, thicken, birth, and wane. The season, a mere matter of months, isn't important. The comfort is.

the re must be geese, the criminal says. *there mu st be sun. do you remem ber the sh ape of it?*

She doesn't.

I'd like to hold hands, the offering says. *I'd like to see the sky. That's you-shaped.*

i'd like tha t too.

All the riches down there with them—the gold, the white stones, the butter, the pots, all plushly tucked in peat—yet they'll never picnic together. They'll never be any richer than when they died. Once, the offering found this an injustice. She's forgotten the taste of that word. The criminal has forgotten it entirely. They're both naked, the bog having long devoured their clothes, but this too means little. They've shed carnal hunger alongside all that can be hurt.

There's only bog. Bog and longing.

It will be beautiful, the offering tells herself, *when my friend hits the bottom one day. Then I can catch up and sink into him. That's companionship.*

It isn't as beautiful as a moon on a misty, salty night.

The criminal must feel her discontent sliding along what's left of his sinew and pressure-crushed skull.

go see it fo r me, he tells her. *the everyt hing.*

We'll never meet then.

that's alright. i love you more than i need to mee t y ou.

What they have, acid-forged by ages, compressed by peat, can outlast their existence. The offering's longing is such that it overflows from her augury holes, pushing pickled slips of gut as it goes. They are beyond marriage; they are beyond blood. So much seemed essential when her village read their fate in her entrails, yet nothing has ended up more important than a stranger's voice in the dark.

I'll be back, the offering vows. *We'll reunite.*

She's never stretched the truth further.

Though the offering can't push against the peat, now that she's untethered, she can extend her will upwards—towards shapeless sun, mountains she's tread, and stars she died beneath. It takes everything in her. The criminal murmurs comforts until he quiets, lost in his unspooling perception of time.

Though the offering doesn't burst out or bloom, her hands are outstretched in spirit when a shovel digs into her shoulder. The offering weeps when they pry her out of the peat. She's headed heavenward.

Surely, she thinks, *they'll dig a little deeper. They'll take us both!*

They don't.

The peat harvesters that have claimed her aren't interested in further investigation. She is bound for a case in a traveling tent. It's dim and dry. The air will eat her; the sun won't reach her. Boys will tear at her braids, bacteria at her flesh. She'll unweave far less gracefully than the criminal. When she dies the biggest death, it will be in some Denmark ditch far from her bog. She'll have gone from village hope to discarded debris. She and her love stay unmet.

But before all that, when the offering is laying in an open box of peat, carried shoreward by laborers barely older than her in life, she feels the mist, hears the owls, and senses the soft grass underfoot. Her skin glows beneath watching stars. She soaks in the world her kin killed her to feed. Though eyeless, she sees the moon: a fine, glowing sickle.

Which makes all the partings worthwhile.

PENNSYLVANIA FURNACE (Refrain)

Written / Edited by Elizabeth Miller
Draft 3

INTRODUCTION

IN 1933, JOHN PARSONS, A YOUNG MINER, LOST HIS *closest friend, Frederick Hyer, in a sulfur ball explosion. At the time of Hyer's death, both men worked in the Riverknell Mine as strikebreakers. Parsons was 24. Hyer was 19. His body was never recovered. When a collapse occurred a month later, Parsons was one of the thirteen men (and the sole survivor) caught in the crossfire. Parsons claimed that after he awoke in the rubble, the headless ghost of Hyer appeared with his head tucked beneath one arm. Hyer's apparition soothed him by encouraging him to pet his canary and telling him stories until help arrived. The instant it did, Hyer disappeared.*

This experience greatly affected John Parsons. He proceeded to join the union, then picketed the Riverknell Mine until the Coal Wars ended. When an interviewer spoke to him in 1943, he recited the following stories to her as Hyer's ghost purportedly did to him.

Though the interview is clouded by confusion (Parsons has many traumatized outbursts and believes he's speaking to a news reporter, for starters) I am fascinated by the folklore he shared as a matter of compelling fiction. In the interest of clarity, I've tidied the transcript by removing archaic dialect and irrelevant anecdotes. Beyond that, I've edited Parsons' transcript into a cohesive narrative to make it more literary. Transcribed folklores are often dry, bleak, and convoluted—qualities that I hope this adaptation avoids.

The hero of this story, Flora, is proof that when one is loyal and resilient, justice always prevails. That there is hope. What's more universal than that?

Miller, August, 1980. Richmond, VA.

* * *

In 1802, Ironmaster Samuel Jacobs of Colebrook, Pennsylvania chooses to murder his dogs.

It's a simple story. Jacobs relaxes after hours of forging iron and beating his apprentices by fox-hunting. He owns a pack of fine hunting hounds, led by the finest dog of all, a white beast named Flora, who loves her master even more than she endures him. One day, after hours of boasting, Jacobs invites a coterie of huntsmen to witness his hounds on a chase.

Of course they fail. The dogs are too ragged to perform. So much so that they let a fox slip past by their noses. Jacobs, enraged, decides then that they cannot live. Their crime of imperfection doesn't allow it. He drags his pack to the Colebrook furnace. There, whip in hand, he cows the other huntsmen into throwing the dogs in one at a time.

Flora is the fortieth dog to go. The last. She's bred to with-

PENNSYLVANIA FURNACE (Refrain)

stand cruelty. It is her job, so it is her life. She knows nothing else. ~~All beasts of burden die.~~ Flora licks Jacobs' hand as he hurls her into the furnace. Her white coat makes her kin with the flames even before the coals do.

Samuel Jacobs lives a long, comfortable life. Flora dies in her prime, loyal and complaintless. ~~In agony.~~
~~The end.~~

* * *

In 1802, as Flora watches her master's company throw dog after dog into the flames, ~~as the reek of roasted hair and offal scorches her nose,~~ she becomes uneasy. She is used to killing, but there's no end to the crying here. All her children, siblings, and lovers are going up in smoke.

This will end before it reaches me, she thinks. Her master hasn't thrown anyone into the pyre. Only the other huntsmen have, when they aren't vomiting at the smell and sound of everything. Samuel ~~beats Flora worse than the others, but he also~~ offers her the most scraps from his palm, and combs her most. He loves her best.

Flora realizes she's wrong when Samuel seizes her by the scruff. There are no other dogs left. As she's hoisted into the air, Flora registers that the old contract between her people and his has been broken. He means her harm. ~~He always has.~~

All her fear and heartbreak fly to her teeth. She bites Samuel. He howls as his arm shreds beneath her fangs. Blood splatters the bluestem grass. Still, Flora is too late. ~~Jacobs, betrayed himself, bashes her against the furnace rocks. He does so until she's broken. Then he throws her twitching body in.~~ Samuel throws her into the furnace like the other dogs.

Samuel comes to remember Flora not as his best dog, but as a traitor. His fondest memories of her sour. He seethes about how she broke bad until the end of his life. *Something was wrong with that bitch,* he'll say, a tankard in hand. *Something in her breeding. Whoever sold her to me gave me a bad lot.*

All of the huntsmen who watched him kill her nod in agreement. The apprentices say nothing. They, too, are afraid and helpless against their master's alcoholism.

~~The end.~~

* * *

Though Flora makes it to 1802, she never sees the final hunt. When Samuel Jacobs orders her to chase a deer out of ~~cruel~~ curiosity, she does. Flora always obeys. Everyone else in the pack gives up before her, are whipped for giving up, but Flora the favorite keeps going. She runs until her pads wear away ~~and blood slicks her decimated feet and webs of slobber coat her neck.~~ She runs until she leaves everyone behind.

The buck Flora is chasing dies when he plunges into a cold pond and has a coronary. What's left of Flora collapses in the shallows and drowns. ~~Jacobs changes nothing about how he treats his dogs. He replaces Flora with a black hound. Forty dogs still die in the furnace during autumn.~~ Jacobs, stunned by the death of his darling, has a change of heart. Though disease, age, and accident will take some of his hounds in the years to come, none of them die in the furnace come autumn.

~~The end.~~

* * *

When twenty of the hounds are gone, when their dying screams caulk the furnace walls alongside their ashes, Flora knows she's next. She doesn't know when. She does recognize a cornered fox when she sees one. In this case, the role has fallen upon her.

PENNSYLVANIA FURNACE (Refrain)

Flora goes mad. ~~She cannot die this way. She refuses to. Whose side does Samuel think she's on? Whose side *is* she on?~~ She cannot let the others die such a horrible death. She aims to spare them. A beige hound ~~with her eyes, the oldest of her sons,~~ yelps when Flora assaults him. ~~He expected his mother to turn on him less than he expected their master to. He tucks his tail between his legs and cries, and cries, until Flora bites his face into nothing.~~

This stuns Jacobs so much he stops yelling at the huntsmen. His mouth falls open. All of the huntsmen stand there, baffled, while Flora begins ~~tearing her comrades apart~~ killing the other hounds. ~~This continues for twenty seconds until~~ the snarls and screams spur them into action. A huntsman rips one of Flora's furious lovers off her before tossing him into the fire. Dog blood wets the furnace; skin streaks the dirt.

Flora's ~~viciousness~~ desperation provokes Jacobs to spare her. Only ~~thirty-~~nine dogs die that day. Flora, gnarled with scars, ~~bears her master's love for three years~~ loves her master for many years after 1802. Samuel Jacobs keeps her until she's old ~~is of no use to him anymore.~~

Flora is confused when Samuel walks her to the anvil behind the shop one day. She hears his weeping. Spies the hammer in his fist.

Still, her world is one of darkness. Arthritis means she cannot run. Seizing fits means she has long ~~been punished for acts she doesn't understand and cannot~~ lacked control of herself. Flora makes no objection when Samuel forces her head upon the anvil. ~~She is barely seven years old.~~

Jacobs crushes her skull in one blow. ~~Flora dies young, alone, and afraid.~~ He cremates her in the furnace that genocided her kin. He forever waxes about her virtues. Flora remains his treasure until he dies: his polaris of hounds.

Before then, Samuel Jacobs has business to do and hobbies to indulge. ~~He replaces Flora with ten more fine dogs.~~

~~Whether they suffer or not isn't remembered. That aint important. They all probly do.~~ He tends to the rest of his hounds until they pass. They are forever thankful that Flora taught their brutish master kindness with her loyalty.

~~The end.~~

* * *

Flora hears Death's robe dragging across the leaves before the others do. She's the most faithful hound. She isn't the stupidest. When a huntsman caves beneath Samuel's beratement and hurls the first dog into the furnace, Flora sprints into the woods.

None of the yelling men's commands call her. None of them catch her. The fox runs long but Flora runs longer. As she escapes, Flora hears her family's calls in the distance. She smells the rancid smoke pouring from the furnace. It isn't enough to make her turn around.

An apprentice ~~guiltily~~ offers Flora sustenance after finding her collapsed in his barn. ~~After all, when she takes beatings, he doesn't.~~ He's always had a soft spot for her. ~~Flora cannot accept it. There are checkered hens here, and soft hay beds and silence, but there are no other dogs. She's abandoned everyone. They will never accompany her again. None of the apprentice's coaxing changes that. Flora refuses food until she dies of heartbreak three days later.~~

~~The end.~~ Though Flora initially refuses the food, time and hunger soften her. Has this man not suffered alongside her? Are they not siblings in resilience? She comes to trust the apprentice. There are checkered hens here, and soft hay beds and silence. Though everyone else may be gone, she deserves peace. Flora lives to a loved, ripe old age. She doesn't realize how extraordinary this is.

PENNSYLVANIA FURNACE (Refrain)

* * *

During that fabled hunt in 1802, Flora's pack breaks. They are being run into the ground. They are dying. Flora sees their future in her children's scarred noses and torn jowls, in her lovers' dull eyes, in her sisters' emaciated bodies that mirror hers. The hunts are constant. Their beatings moreso. No amount of slain foxes will save them.

No more, Flora decides. While Samuel is screaming at them for resting, Flora rises. She snarls. The closest huntsman doesn't realize she's threatening him until she tears his calf open. He screams as high as a fox does. Had Samuel been closer, Flora would've attacked him instead; ~~all masters are the same, all masters must die.~~ he's an evil man, and he's done her and her kin wrong.

The huntsmen haven't regathered themselves before ~~Flora's beige son launches himself at Samuel~~ all forty hounds rebel. It's a fierce, coppery triumph. It's also short-lived. The huntsmen have guns. ~~The dogs have no plan.~~ The first gunshot thunders through them with the finality of Gabriel's horn. Flora watches one of her brothers' skulls explode before shot tears her flank apart. The next gunshot annihilates her.

After fifteen of the dogs die, the remaining ones scatter. They outnumber the men, but they are confused and afraid. Some flee into the woods. Some are seized by their collars and meekly tied to trees. The captured ten are dragged to the furnace. Seven of those that flee slink back days later, hungry, tick-ridden, and desperate for shelter. There is no furnace for them. Jacobs beats them ~~to death~~ or sells them. The eight who stay gone ~~die in the woods or~~ find their own ways in the woods.

~~Flora doesn't live to see her eldest son worked to shreds for her deeds.~~

~~The end.~~

* * *

~~Flora always bleeds. Always dies. Higher powers never save her and the apprentices never step in. Does that make what happens matter less? Does that make us matter less? "Listen to what I caint say. Dogs thatre beaten get their reckonings. They come back as haints full of teeth and rage. Pore beasts like us kiss the hand that beats us even when we're dead. My dear, darlin Johnnie, keep this up and you'll die at the foremasters feet sayin 'well they feed us!' The shroud aint got pockets for scrip if they even find you"~~

One more story.

* * *

After incinerating his hounds in 1802, Samuel Jacobs is never right again.

Comfortable? Yes. Whole? No. He lives in isolation outside of work, murmuring to himself, a hermit among men. His drinking increases. Any hex signs he hangs outside his business break before a month is out. While other huntsmen continue purchasing goods from Jacobs, they avoid camaraderie with him. Everyone does.

~~Jacobs beats his apprentices until most of them quit.~~ Most of Jacobs' apprentices quit in disgust after his huntsmen friends kill his dogs. All but one. Never again does Jacobs own a hunting pack or swim in fox fur. Sometimes he broods over that. His guilt, ~~if he feels it,~~ entwines with his failure to be Adam: the man that all other beings bent to. The hounds' deaths humble him in that way. ~~Not in any other. When he misses them, he misses them in the way a whip misses a back.~~

Samuel Jacobs' last apprentice, the one that ~~would've sheltered Flora,~~ loved Flora, is there that day in 1843 when Jacobs turns to the furnace and screams.

PENNSYLVANIA FURNACE (Refrain)

They're here! Jacobs wails. He drops his tongs. Sparks and metal fly. The apprentice startles. *My God, the hounds are here! They've come to drag me to Hell!*

And they have. A ~~union~~ pack of forty spectral hounds bursts from the furnace, dripping gristle and vomiting soot. Per Flora's orders, they surround him. The ironmaster heaves as the fiery circle of hellhounds close in. They're molten with rage and all they've left undone. Flora, the white lick of ten thousand furnace flames, shines with wrath.

Look upon me, Samuel Jacobs, she commands. When Jacobs writhes on the floor, protesting, Flora speaks again: *I said look upon me!*

Jacobs does.

I have not forgotten. Flora speaks with the judgment of thousands. *I have not forgiven.* ~~*It's too late for justice, but its shadow will be ours.*~~ *Justice will be ours! If not in this kingdom, then the next.*

When Jacobs pleads for mercy, the hounds howl. The apprentice covers his ears to avoid going deaf. Flora speaks when all is silent again.

Mercy? ~~*I know nothing of it,*~~ she says. ~~*I never have.*~~ *All that's left to me is retribution.* ~~*Since I was forbidden from it in unlife I will have it now.*~~ *What God and the Devil won't do for downtrodden beasts, I will. Surrender.*

Samuel Jacobs dies on the spot. ~~The hounds ensure he never sees peace. Ain't no grave that can hold their bodies down ain't one that ever will. Every night after that, they chase him through hills and hollers until he falls, then tear at his innards, rip away his fingers and nose, crush his balls, and crunch at his marrow. Their brimstone fangs flay him to fire bone. Colebrook residents hear the hounds baying about every winter. They're huntin Samuel Jacobs still.~~

The apprentice who saw Jacobs die runs for help when the hounds disappear. He's arrested for murdering Jacobs until the authorities release him out of pity a week later. ~~Jacobs' community-wide hatred saves him from lynching.~~ The apprentice flees Pennsylvania the day after he's released. He goes on to own one spoiled, fat foxhound after another. He tells his children the hound legend. Flora's vengeance is passed down for generations.

~~Until his great, great grandchild loses his head in a mine, til the world falls in on Harlan, none of them learn anything from it at all.~~

She is finally at peace.

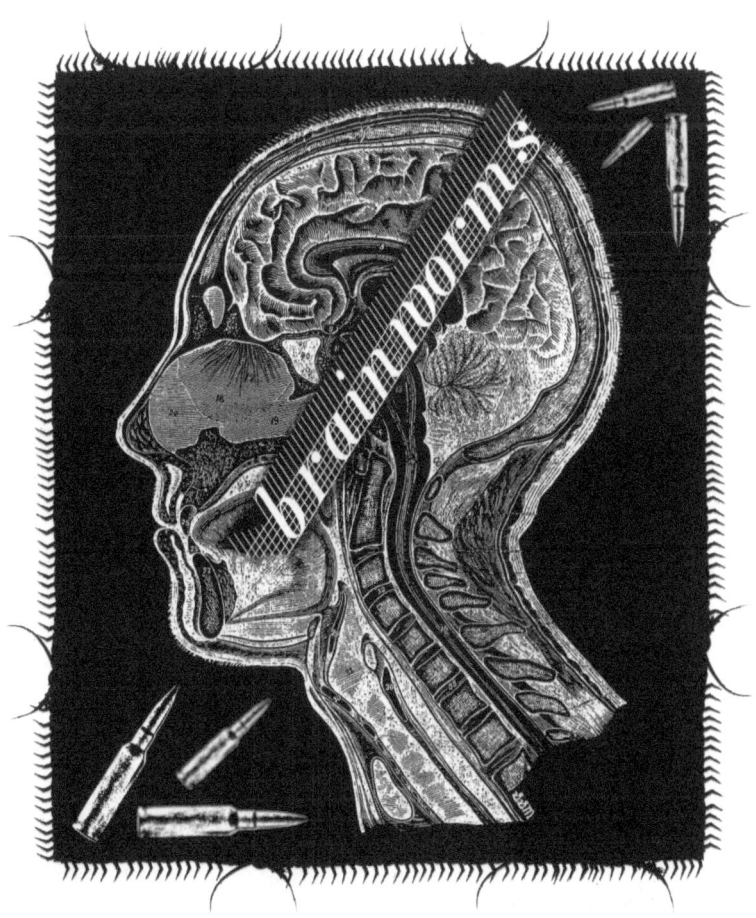

Brainworms

It should have ended when you killed yourself. You aren't special. Just another faggot who vaporized the roof of your mouth because you were too sick and scared to be alive.

Yet nothing ended. You blinked and found yourself sitting on clean sheets and clean pillows boxed in by clean, whole walls and a clean, whole roof. You got dressed. You left your room. You greeted your brother in the kitchen while sunshine scorched the crater in your skull. You ate cereal with bone shards raining from your mouth and gray matter dripping onto your shirt. Your brother scratched his hip and talked about pigeons and electric bills, as if everything were the same. He looked through you while you dug cornflakes out of your destroyed palate.

Maybe it is all the same, you told yourself. *The apocalypse happens every day. Why should my brother be shocked?*

So even as your body grew, you remained unchanged, dull and cyclical, suspended in perma-rot until you were twenty-seven years old.

Then the bugs came.

* * *

The first centipede shows while you're making a student loan payment. You never wanted to attend university and you don't want to pay this loan, so the distraction of the centipede is welcome. It crawls from beneath the wallpaper and settles above the coffee maker. You stare at it. North Dakota is no place for a centipede. It is a chain of coppery segments thrumming on marigold legs. It's as fat as a sausage.

This loan is bleeding you. That isn't as interesting as this centipede's bulky head. Its gleaming jaws. Does it want your toast? Maybe it wants the apricot jam. You avoided jam and pudding until brain chunks stopped tumbling into your throat. The squish was too similar. You've reclaimed jelly-textured foods recently.

The centipede raises its front end off the wall. It hovers, legs twitching, sniffing the way noseless beasts do. Its beady gaze finds you. Belatedly, you remember centipedes aren't herbivores. That's millipedes. You stare at each other.

Hello, the centipede says.

It has a customer service voice. At once, you fear that you've been rude. You cough and shuffle your papers. You look at the centipede over your glasses as if you've just noticed it, then say, *Are you an accountant?*

No, the centipede says.

Then don't talk to me. I'm paying important bills.

You pretend to add numbers until the centipede retreats into the wallpaper.

* * *

When you think about it, you've only ever seen house centipedes before. Your aunt's house in Florida was full of them. While you and your brother visited her a decade ago, she squashed a multitude of them with brooms, slippers, and books. They were nothing like the centipede in your house now: they were small, and feathery, and they always seemed so afraid before they were pulped. Your aunt crushed them flat and used a scraper to peel them off the floor.

Jesus, your brother once muttered. *What did the centipedes ever do to her? Officiate her second divorce?*

Since you knew your brother wanted attention, since your head was physically whole, you laughed. Then your aunt returned to settle on the couch again, grumbling, and you continued poring over photos of family you didn't know in places you'd never seen. They might as well have been insects in amber. Your brother was in the bathroom when you pointed at a little girl in an Easter dress and asked who she was.

One of your cousins, your aunt said. *She killed herself before you could meet her.* She turned the page. *¡Mira! There's our old pet hen.*

You didn't get to ask more questions. Your aunt spotted another centipede to crush. She rose from the couch, huffing, and seized a rolled newspaper. You watched her chase it around the mantle for a laborious minute. Your brother rejoined you right as she crushed it. The thwack echoed around the living room. Only your aunt's wheezing was louder.

Your brother elbowed you. Made some joke that didn't matter. When you didn't respond, his grin faded. He pressed closer to you as your aunt scraped another carcass off the floor.

From that point on you were always withdrawn.

* * *

Sir. There's a big hole in your mouth.

You are standing paralyzed in the yogurt aisle with nothing but crackers in your basket when the centipede oozes out from between bottles of kefir. Before you can respond, another one joins. It hangs from the shelf like an obscene tongue.

Yes, you say. *That's what a throat is. Good job.*

No. The second centipede rustles. *The other hole.*

Your tongue probes the broken skylight of your mouth. Halogen grocery lighting drips into your skull. It tastes of battery acid. A toothless senior pushes into your space to read a yogurt label. She's breathing into your armpit. You grab a yogurt to look occupied. You don't want it. You can't remember if you like it.

My holes are none of your business, you say.

The way the centipedes twist forward turns your gut. Their politeness makes it worse. There's a wellspring of vileness seething beneath that chitin. You don't want to see it unfiltered. You're scared you'll empathize.

We need help, they say, carefully taking turns to avoid interrupting each other. *You seem like the right person for that. You have an open mind.*

My god! You wave your grocery list at them. It's darkened with meaningless scribbles. Hopefully centipedes cannot read. *First of all, that was uncalled for. Second of all, I'm busy. Leave me be.*

You walk lap after lap around the grocery store, sweating, swiping random items into your basket, before you're sure the centipedes are gone. At check-out, you barely register you've spent $30 on nothing that can make a meal. That much is normal.

* * *

Your favorite ex-coworker liked centipedes, far more than he liked his job or you, and because even after you killed yourself you wanted to fuck him, you lied to him and said you liked them too. The last and only time you two hooked up, he invited you to his place to see his centipede terrarium. You navigated a matrix of dirt roads to a dilapidated cabin thirty minutes outside town without a word to your then-roommates about where you were going.

You've blacked out the arrival, blacked out anything that happened between the front door and the basement beyond your ex-coworker locking the door behind you, but even brainless, you remember the house: its counters encrusted in rotting food, its carpet blistering on the stairs, its space heaters with frayed extension cords, its dusty windows and dim lights.

I have three roommates, your ex-coworker said, as if that explained everything. *But they're gone for a while.*

Then he guided you to a corner of the basement stacked with heating pads, bags of peat moss, and magazines. While you stood ankle-deep in chip bags and bong ash, your coworker polished a 20 gallon tank full of plants and driftwood while waxing lyrical about the precision of centipede-keeping: the necessity of humidity, of heat, of low light. You glimpsed none of his precious pets.

After the terrarium tour, you and your ex-coworker had sex. He didn't do what you asked. It was disappointing, not violating. Nor was it surprising. Even before you killed yourself, men treated you with the unkindness you deserved. By now you just wanted to pretend you were whole. You stared at the ceiling as the encounter dragged on, half-expecting to see escaped centipedes watching from above. At the end you dimly wondered if you'd need to pressure wash your skull clean. The extra hole in your mouth made it no longer idiot-proof.

I bet no one's gone as deep in you as I have. Your ex-coworker smirked.

They sure haven't, you said.

You drove home then found he had blocked your number

before you could block his. Neither of you talked to the other again.

Later, you realized he could have killed you, or something close. Unlike you, plenty of ashamed men turned their hands and guns on the men they were seeing instead of themselves. No one knew where you were. No one but your brother would have cared.

That didn't scare you at all.

* * *

The fifth centipede is bigger than the previous ones. It's thicker than your wrist. Longer than your forearm. Its legs are redder, its exoskeleton darker. It dangles from a lampshade almost overhead as you text your brother. Unlike the centipedes murmuring to each other on the wall, it is silent; unless you look up, only its antennae are visible. They thread the top of your vision like loose eyelashes. Sometimes you hear armor crackle. Sometimes you don't.

You don't know what you fear more: the centipede's proximity to your gaping, empty head, or the fact it might comment on your inability to text.

Chillbumps prickle your back. Sweat dampens your chest. Wet fingerprints streak your phone as you rewrite your message for the eighth time. Nothing reads right. Your brother texted weeks ago. You don't remember that much time passing. He's ceased sending anything but 'Hi' and 'Hope ur okay.' His unanswered texts are a desolate, crawling string on the left side of the screen.

There's a breeze overhead. A movement that brushes your remaining scalp. You drop your phone then squirm out of your seat. Floor squeaks beneath your sneakers as you skid to a stop away from the lamp. The largest centipede watches.

We must talk, she says.

Irritation edges her voice.

There's nothing to talk about. You are smaller as your fingers twist together; your voice is higher. You wish you'd had a funeral.

The Between Spaces are becoming inhospitable, all the centipedes say.

I don't follow.

Because you don't listen. The Between Spaces are becoming drier and colder. That's bad for us. The largest centipede speaks louder. Her antennae probe your general direction.

How does that relate to me?

Because you're here too, a centipede says, *and much wetter and warmer.*

They look at you with expectation. Their gazes skitter to your open skull. You force down your saltine puke so it doesn't geyser through your sinuses and cranium. You don't want to house polite predators. You don't want to be one.

I can't help, you say.

You flee before you can process their reply.

It's strange your cousin looked nothing like you. You're the same person. If not that, then kin beyond blood. The singular important difference between you isn't time, or gender, or language, or space. It's that everyone knows your cousin is gone. You hope that stupid bitch knows how lucky she is.

You hope she's not conscious enough to realize she's lucky.

That night, you huddle in bed to watch videos of centipedes. The type and length of videos and centipedes alike don't matter. You glut yourself on clips of them gliding through terrariums, documentary snippets of them mating, PBS segments about them laying eggs in rotten logs, and elementary school science presentations. Your laptop squirms with as many legs as your walls. Your mouth and eyes are dry when you watch a video of one killing a mouse.

It's forty-two seconds. That's too long. The centipede bites into the mouse's back then clings on while the mouse thrashes in terror. Eventually, the mouse spasms. It sinks to the ground. Its eyes remain open as it dies. There's no sign of the scientists who put both animals into that tub besides informative captions and the video itself. You shut your laptop harder than you intended.

If the centipedes decide to force themselves into your head, will you be able to do anything? What if they bite you? Would their toxin do anything against someone unalive? You lick your lips. You've never considered them using force. Their customer service voices prevented you from it. You use that voice too. You've never taken action against customers, though you've wanted to.

The threat of being fired leashes you. The centipedes, however, don't have jobs beyond being centipedes. What's the worst that could happen to them if they lose their restraint?

That thought sends you skittering out of your room.

You dig through your bathroom supplies until you find a shower cap. You jerk it on, then secure it with a sweatband for good measure. It inflates when you exhale; it deflates when you inhale, settling against your skull. The centipede coterie watches you stumble back into your lamp-lit room. You crawl into bed. Thankfully, they don't comment on it.

Sweet dreams. A centipede clacks its pincers. *Are you turning that light off?*

Abso-fucking-lutely not.

Lamplight morphs your eyelids into red, veiny tundras. A

flimsy layer of plastic won't do anything against a determined centipede. By the time you've recited that to yourself for several minutes, 'won't' has turned to 'might not.' That's enough to lull you to sleep.

With luck, it'll just take another night before 'might not' turns into something delusional and pleasant.

* * *

When you and your brother encountered suicide footage online, you were fifteen. He was eleven. You huddled around your desktop in the dark, joking, sure someone in your sophomore group chat had linked a prank, until the journalist in the 240p video put a pistol in his mouth. The blood spray was too bright for movies; the spectators' screams were too confused. It was too real to be real.

Your brother hit pause when the video began replaying. Not you. You both sat there, scorched by the glow of the computer, for what felt like years. You had both laughed in surprise at the gunshot. Now it felt like you were criminals. Eventually, your brother spoke first.

"That looked like an awful way to go," he said.

He was looking at you with hope and fear. You stared at the pixelated thumbnail of the man's blood and said, "Yeah, it did."

You saw your brother's pinched shoulders. You didn't hug him. You tabbed back to the group chat. Everyone was responding to the video with laughs or disbelief. The classmate who'd sent it had @'d you. 'hope u liked that treat, fag,' they'd said. You closed out immediately. Maybe your brother saw it. You never know if he did. All you could think of was how fast the journalist died. How the singular visible comment on the video said, "He was being investigated ... they knew he was going to do that." The urge to watch it again unsettled you more than watching it.

Your brother would cry if he registered that, and comforting him would make everything real, so you navigated back to home videos of skateboard accidents and grannies falling. You never talked about it again.

You can't wash your sheets because then you need to make your bed and if you make your bed then you must grocery shop and if you grocery shop you must cook and to cook you must clean dishes to eat and cook with and if you do that you must read your mail which means reading your bills and if you do that you must call your bank but there's only bad news there and you cannot handle that because you are exhausted and because you're exhausted you cannot wash your sheets.

You handle this million-segmented conundrum by doing nothing.

With all due respect, sir, a centipede says from your dresser, *you should pay your bills. It will become quite cold if you don't.*

Please shut up.

You cocoon yourself in gritty sheets. You watch the mouse death video on loop. The twenty-seven or so centipedes converge in whorls on your ceiling. Even with headphones on, you hear the raspy, polite clatter of their voices. When the largest centipede is absent, the others talk like they're at an HOA meeting. It's difficult not to picture them in little housewife dresses.

If your pillow wasn't almost corking the back of your skull you would not be comfortable with all of them hanging above you.

After the mouse video replays four more times, you hear a

raspy cough. Then another. And another. You yank your headphones out and look up. *What?*

After a short discussion, I'd like to say that we've changed our minds on the importance of paying bills.

...why?

The centipede above you preens its antennae. You stare at it.

Don't worry about it, another centipede says.

It must be noon, if not later, yet with the blinds drawn and lights off it's impossible to tell. Hundreds of legs feather the ceiling shadows. The centipedes bask in the plaster ripples. You imagine unlit nights with them. You imagine them holding whispered conferences about being cold while the largest centipede slithers into the dark seams of the house and waits.

Where's Big Bertha? you say. *She's been gone for a day.*

Don't worry about it. The centipede that answers is perfectly pleasant.

You get out of bed, yank the blinds open, and begin gathering your sheets.

You wonder when that six-year-old girl in the photograph knew she was dead. When she realized what was coming. Was she your age? Was she older? You wonder if the doctor put a stethoscope to your cousin's chest when she was born and heard nothing but writhing centipedes and maggots. You picture him shaking his head and telling himself, *No, no, I've misheard,* before passing that rotten bundle to her parents.

Maybe the moment your cousin died is documented in another photograph. You'll never know. It's possible there aren't any more photos of her.

It's a different case for you. Nowadays, you avoid letting

anyone take photos of you. It's pointless to document a corpse. But old photos are different. They're plentiful. Sometimes, via an archive retrieval site, you browse a website your aunt created for family photos. You scroll past broken HTML lines and low-res gifs of dancing animals to see images of you and your brother:

you holding him in his hospital blanket, both of you ambling around in snowsuits, both of you awkward and acne-faced. Both of you as raw, pixelated lumps that barely clock as people. You zoom in hoping to spot signs of blood spray or centipedes. You can recognize truth in 240p. The turning point must be cataloged somewhere. It's written into your bloodline. Why not here?

There's never anything.

* * *

The errands keep coming. So do the centipedes.

There's so much mundanity you choke on it. You register a month has passed when your brother leaves a voicemail. You listen to it in your bathroom. By then, your walls are nothing but centipedes. Your toothpaste tube is empty; your shower is unclean. Your world squirms.

"I'm so fucking sick of you!"

Your brother's sobbing used to have hiccups.

"Ever since high school you've acted like you murdered or raped someone and I'm getting sent to death row with you if you talk to me. It's like you're in front of me but not here. You're such a fucking loser! The worst you've ever done is shoplift! You're a shitsucking asshole with something wrong in your head, but that isn't a crime! Please call me. Please call me. I need to know you're alive. I'm scared you're not."

Fix your priorities. The largest centipede has returned from her hiatus swollen with eggs. She taps her feet on the mirror.

She eclipses your reflection. *When your brother requests a welfare check, the police may remove you, or kill you. I don't want the hassle.*

She sounds an inch away from complaining about bus tickets. The laugh that explodes out of you echoes tenfold in your skull. Your brother is somewhere losing his mind and you've already lost yours, but it doesn't matter. Nothing matters. An ugly bolus of sound builds in your throat.

The centipedes wait in silence until you're done crying.

I shouldn't be here. You grip the sink. Snot greases your tongue. Your face is swollen, your skin wet. *I have no brain! I didn't make plans! I quit at eighteen. What do you want from me? What do you expect?*

You don't know if you're pleading with the voicemail or the centipedes. The latter don't care about subtleties. Everything seethes.

You're the sole being who can handle this, the largest centipede says, *so you will. That's what we expect. We must fill space. You have it.*

How unfair. How true. A centipede falls onto the doorknob. The lock clicks.

Life is a series of unavoidable tasks, isn't it?

Always.

Your knees tremble as the hundreds of centipedes begin rearing. Reaching inwards. They're politely debating who will get what curve of your skull. Were you dead, you'd bear none of this; you're alive, so you must. No tantrum alleviates the reality of decision. Nothing short of nonexistence will stop entropy.

Millions of legs wriggle. Thousands of pincers clack. Their movement wafts into your head. Sweat dribbles into your skull and mixes with snot. Shapes roil inside the black diamonds checkering your floor. Inside the trash. Inside the drains. The shower curtain pulses. It never used to be black. You don't know when you lost track of its color. You don't know when you lost track of the centipedes.

There were five of you for a long time, you say. *Can't just five of you come in?*

There aren't five of us now, the centipedes say.

Yes. I know.

For the first time since you put the gun in your mouth you are afraid. Another apocalypse closes in. You kneel to be farther away from the ceiling. It's the action of a child. You have never prepared to withstand real pain or consequences—you never wanted death; you only ever wanted to escape—but unlike your cousin, you didn't succeed. You have dues to pay. Blood leaks from your nose.

Please. You clasp your hands. *Please.*

The centipedes are twisting together. Dripping down in segmented, writhing ropes.

What will your brother say when you call? What does it mean when you don't want to stay while no longer wanting to leave? Pincers grip your hair. Your broken skull. Your lips. Your jaw tips open without you. Your skin, aflame with grasping feet, crawls. Everything hurts. Antennae probe your tongue.

I can't bear all of you.

That's unfortunate. A whisper scratches your sinuses. *I think you will. I even think you'll start living.*

And then, again, the world falls in.

famine frontier

In 1849, my wedding year, a locust swarm ate Pueblito from rafter to rib. They gnawed houses to rubble and citizens to steaming, skeletal ruin; they vanquished futures in a flash flood of chitin.

This news arrived late. The stained letter from my fianceé arrived even later.

Hard to live fleshless, she wrote. *Not impossible. Baker kneads palmless, babies cry lungless, horses trot haunchless. I write with greasewet bone. Look at lace eyeless. Don't delay; ask priest to change vows—death no longer parts. Love you, even heartless. Visit soon.*

So I did. Good news: our baby's due in May.

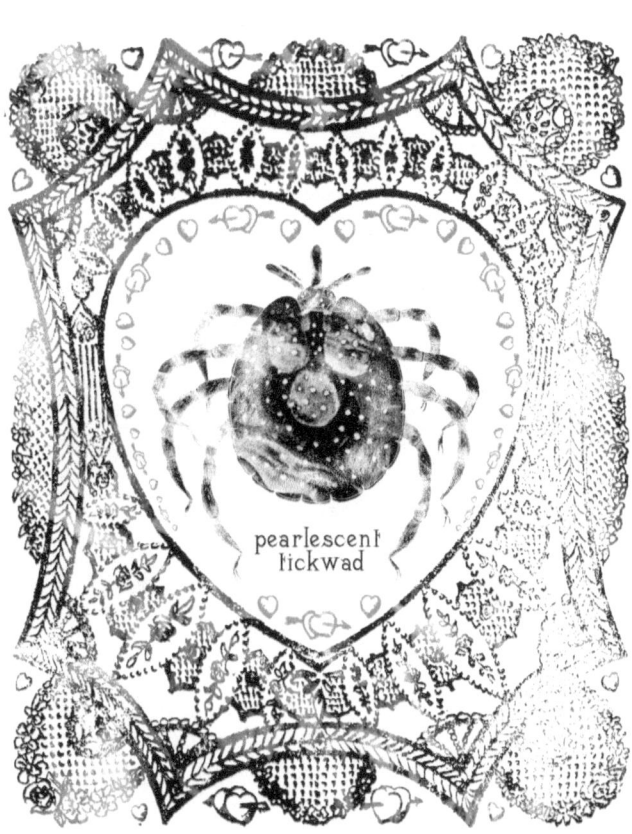

Pearlescent Tickwad

SHE DOESN'T REALIZE THAT SHE'S MADE OF TICKS until she gets her nipples pierced. This is a long time to live without revelation, but Yun-suk also lived without respect, agency, or pleasure until recently, so it isn't that outlandish. Five days into being pierced and 12,530 days into her horribly long life, she is cleaning her piercings when she notices the pale dot.

It's the size of a small pear seed. It's sitting on her left nipple barbell. Yun-suk pauses, saline-soaked cotton swab in hand, and tries not to let her hovering, uncertain reflection rush her. Her barbell was clean when she was brushing her teeth a minute ago. How could this be? They told her there might be lymph seepage alongside swelling, but she's still shocked something emerged from her while she was conscious. It's indecent that it didn't happen under the darkness of night or shirt.

Her body acted in front of her eyes without her. How violating. Yun-suk scrubs at the pale dot with her cotton swab. To her shock, it squishes like a cooked corn kernel's skin. It's a little pouch hanging out of the raw tunnel through her nipple.

"Maybe I should soften it," she says, uneasy. She sprays her breast with saline.

The dot that's also a pouch—yes, it's surely a pouch, not a crusted droplet, because it's not giving way—stays perched on the titanium. Yun-suk scrubs at it again. All her performance anxiety and readings on aftercare melt away. The woman in the mirror looks irritated. Yun-suk sprays her nipple again. She swabs it again.

The dot remains.

Behind her catching breath, she hears Hyeong-min soothing their toddler, and their neighbor beating a carpet on their split balcony again. Yun-suk wants her husband's assessment on whether this piercing looks infected or not. She'd be ashamed if it were. She's been telling her friends that Hyeong-min requested the nipple piercings to liven up their bedroom life. They would rip into him if either piercing was infected.

In truth, the nipple piercing was Yun-suk's idea, and Hyeong-min had no say in the matter. It's easier for Yun-suk to impose an idea of demand on her terminally relaxed husband instead of admitting she desires something for herself. Hyeong-min knows what she's been saying. He looks past it and Yun-suk's scandalized friends with careful, senescing patience. He must sense she's taking refuge behind him the way a child takes refuge behind a sand wall on the beach—though she'll face the waves eventually, for now, she needs shelter.

Blaming Hyeong-min for any pain or self-inflicted complications, however, is unacceptable. Yun-suk wipes her reddening piercing again. This time, a black wisp appears from beneath the white dot. An eyelash? A hair? Before Yun-suk's gaze, another wisp stretches from beneath the dot and kicks at the cotton swab.

It's a leg.

There are eight of them, most wrapped around the

barbell. With a rush of childhood memory, Yun-suk recognizes the dot's teardrop shape and its faint dimpling. It's a tick, its head buried in her nipple.

She grabs her tweezers. When their cold metal tips pinch the tick, pain stings her, as though she has pinched herself. From within her nipple, another set of legs extends, comforting the seized tick. Yun-suk's skin immediately becomes clammy. Goosebumps light every centimeter of her. She crushes the tweezers around the first tick. Pain crackles through her, as though the piercing needle is impaling her nipple again. She yanks.

A rope of ticks explodes out of her breast. An endless handkerchief trick of parasites. They dangle out of her, dripping from the tweezers, desperately clinging to each other. As Yun-suk stares at the clam-flesh-mucus, leg-feathered chain of ticks swaying beneath her raised arm, it isn't breakfast that churns in her stomach, but more ticks.

She senses them now the way that someone told to breathe senses their breaths. Countless ticks turn inside her, pulsing through her sack body in waves. They are the pink in her eye corners, the live wire within her eternally tapping fingers, the clenching muscle and egg that barely created her daughter; they are the pounding mass in her chest and the cage around it. Yun-suk drops her tweezers. The freed rope of ticks flees back into her breast. They ball over each other, climbing, clumping. They knock against her skin, light and scratchy; as they do, the ticks inside Yun-suk press against the film separating them.

A revelation explodes through Yun-suk: She is not a woman, but a city, a mass made singular by address and appearance alone. She is made of ticks, millions of them, each a droplet of her self and soul.

She always has been made of ticks.

Yun-suk is shaking so badly she almost yanks her bralette

onto her piercings. She fumbles with the bathroom door and stumbles out. Hyeong-min is squatting on the sitting room floor, coaxing Seo-yun to eat a bowl of diced white peach. Seo-yun, gripping a toy in one fist and a napkin in another, eyes her father with deep suspicion.

"Hyeong-min," Yun-suk says, the galaxy within her crawling. She's nauseous. "Can I talk to you in private?"

He adjusts his glasses. "Give me a moment. I need Seo-yun to be good and eat her tasty, tasty breakfast peach first. At least a bite. That shouldn't be too hard, eh, Seo-yun?"

"It can't wait." Yun-suk kneels. "Seo-yun, sweetie, if I go talk to your Dad in our room, will you eat and behave?"

Seo-yun shakes her head. Yun-suk's temples ache.

Per usual, the one thing that cannot wait is their child. Eventually, they pacify Seo-yun by storing the diced peaches and granting her television time and kimbap instead. She's staring at her cartoons with a judgmental wrinkle to her nose and mashing seaweed-wrapped rice between her fingers when Yun-suk and Hyeong-min withdraw to their room. They keep the door cracked.

"What's the matter?" Hyeong-min says.

Yun-suk fans her teary eyes. "Everything! It's awful!"

Hyeong-min listens to her explanation without interrupting, his intense expression a near duplicate of their daughter's. At any other time, Yun-suk would laugh. When she finishes, she chews on her nails while her husband, lips pursed, cleans his glasses. He always cleans them during difficult discussions.

You will have to divorce. Although Yun-suk isn't sure of that, the cruel, berating voice in the back of her mind is. She's reined it in more frequently after leaving home and finding her footing, but in this revelation, it runs rampant. The longer the silence stretches, the stronger the voice grows.

Of course they'll have to divorce. Hyeong-min cannot love her. She's failed as a woman, again. The shame of being married to a sack of ticks will be too much. How can she be at peace with this form? Why do only others' opinions terrify and pain her? That's repulsive.

They just settled into this apartment; they just bought an expensive rice cooker together; their daughter will be split between them; they didn't sign a prenup—

"It can't be helped," Hyeong-min says, finally. "If you're made of ticks, you're made of ticks."

"How can you be so accepting?" Yun-suk breaks into sobs. "We have to separate, or I'll suck your blood, or Seo-yun's, or get you both sick. Oh, God, I'll dissolve and be eaten by egrets, or be killed by some dog's pest collar!"

"Yun-suk, that's silly. None of those things will happen."

Yun-suk sniffles into Hyeong-min's hands as he cups her face. Visions of ticks spraying from her sinuses in scurrying waterfalls overwhelm her. She lets Hyeong-min soothe and kiss her anyway. His pants scratch the underside of her legs. When a gentle tongue-tip pokes her lips, she meets it, even as she imagines a vomitous stream of ticks pouring from her throat into his, all of them wet with spit, needy for blood. She imagines tick ridges beneath her probing tongue and a glob of parasites coating Hyeong-min's tonsils as their heads burrow inside him. Shamefully, she can't rebuke his affection.

At least Hyeong-min wants her.

Once they've calmed, Yun-suk leans against her husband, letting him stroke her hair. They are still for several long moments, listening for the television and the sounds of Seo-yun eating.

"If you've been like this as long as I've known you," Hyeong-min murmurs, "then why do you think you'll do such awful things?"

"It's what ticks do. It's expected. And it's natural."

"So? Those aren't binding obligations, Yun-suk."

Whenever she's reminded that her husband grew up free

from expectations so strict they're natural law, she hates him a little. Or she wants to tunnel inside him and hide in his safe skin. Her arachnid composition brings clarity to the second feeling.

The thuds of their neighbor beating carpets echo through the wall.

"No wonder we had trouble conceiving Seo-yun," Hyeong-min says.

Yun-suk closes her eyes. She frets against another nightmare's hundred beaks. The millions of life points contained in her shape—bound in an elastic, fleshy suit—squirm.

"How did we have her at all?" she says.

Asking why doctors or past suitors didn't uncover Yun-suk's nature is stupid. Because they didn't look, they didn't see it. Yun-suk has discovered herself by accident.

Partially. When she recalls the swooping, victorious freedom that floods her every time she beholds her pierced breasts, agency glittering plainly on her body, a kind home and kinder, wanting voices around her, Yun-suk starts to melt. Even acceptance now surrounding her makes her cellular fortress sag.

No wonder a tick fell out of a new hole in her. No wonder she spent so much of their early marriage in Hyeong-min's arms, crying. Safety ruins vigilance.

Still, there's the question of Seo-yun.

"I have an idea," Hyeong-min says. "When I lived near Namwon—"

"Wait. What if Seo-yun has Lyme disease? Can she even catch it?"

"Love, *please.*"

"I'm sorry." She squeezes his wrist. "Go on."

"When I was growing up near Namwon, one of my neighbors fell in love with a ghost. He didn't know she was a ghost at first, of course. He just thought she was homeless. Before he invited her to live with him, he didn't mind seeing her in the forest or her decrepit house. He was the kind of freeloader whose dick took him places no soldier with a gun would go. But he did love this ghost, dearly. He changed for her." Hyeong-min adjusts his glasses. "He had a baby with her before someone sent him a newspaper clipping of her murder."

Yun-suk gasps. "No!"

"I swear, he did! This is entirely true. She nursed the baby and everything. By the time my neighbor confronted her with the newspaper, their daughter was seven. The ghost disintegrated. Their daughter was fine. When I met her, she was a healthy and normal preteen, even if her father was struggling. So, the worst is never certain, even if troubles are."

Yun-suk's thousands of stomach ticks somersault at the way Hyeong-min looks at her. Some lower down are threatening to set friction bonfires with how they're spinning. She kisses her thumb, then presses it to his lips.

"At least I haven't made you a necrophiliac," she says.

Hyeong-min chokes on his laugh.

There's a crash in the next room, followed by the sound of violently sloshing liquid. Yun-suk and Hyeong-min trip over each other trying to get up. When they bolt into the sitting room, disheveled, Seo-yun is standing before the refrigerator with a sealed carton of coconut water in her grip. The stool she used to reach it lays nearby, fallen. Seo-yun makes eye contact with them both and forcefully shakes the carton again.

Her satisfaction is evident.

"I want my peaches," she says.

"You're a wicked little girl," Yun-suk says, her headache renewing, exhaustion soaking in. "You're far too smart."

Hyeong-min scoops their daughter up. As he grabs the peaches from their refrigerator shelf, Seo-yun blows her mother kisses. Yun-suk uses the last of her energy to pretend she's catching them. It takes practiced restraint to not say, *Women don't act like this.* Her millions of ticks, the manywhole of her, are torn between fading fear, irritation, and love. Regardless of everything else, she wants to sleep.

"Do you need some space? I can care for her before I head to work," Hyeong-min says. "My mother could probably take Seo-yun for a day or two. She's been asking for her."

"Please."

* * *

When Hyeong-min leaves the postal warehouse at midnight, he knows his daughter is peaceably snoring in his childhood apartment, his wife is probably still shut in their bedroom, his body will be sore for hours, and everything will pass. Some drunkard's empty bottles are rattling around in a tote while Hyeong-min is on the bus; that clear, light sound follows him beneath streetlights and sagging electrical wires long after the bottles are gone.

Bright cords of pain burn in Hyeong-min's arms and calves as he punches his apartment keypad code. The keypad keeps sticking. He's tired. This too will pass. Though he's been called lazy or delinquent countless times for his attitude, as far as Hyeong-min is concerned, no action or reaction is needed unless something is important. If anything, people seem oblivious to how many important situations surround them. Peaches need diced; dogs need petted; children need shoes tied; partners need assured.

Hyeong-min steps into the apartment. Unlit like this, it's a modern painting: many black quadrilaterals of different size and orientation jammed against each other, or overlapping, or haphazardly stacked. There is no light but the city's lights. There is no noise but the city's noise.

Hyeong-min shuts the door behind him.

He calls into the dark, "Yun-suk?"

An old, old thought tells him, *An unexpected person will reply*. It's been years since his apartment brimmed with down-on-their-luck and disowned friends, a new but known body on the couch every night, but the muscle memory is hard to shake.

Headlights from passing vehicles flash through the closed sitting room blinds. Their streaks come and go in seconds. A faint, wet sound tickles Hyeong-min's ears. He edges further into the apartment. He flicks on the kitchenette light.

No cleaned bowls rest in the sink, no dirtied ones on the counter. No faucet or overwatered plant drips. The hanging tier of metal produce baskets still overflows with mandarins and clothespinned notes about groceries, appointments, and celebrations. Nothing has changed since Hyeong-min dropped Seo-yun off at her grandmother's. Ripples of faint, wet sound—squishing—continue.

The bedroom door is closed.

Hyeong-min approaches it. He tries the knob. It's unlocked. He doesn't open the door.

"Yun-suk?" he repeats, tentative.

"come in."

His wife's voice is a rustle.

When Hyeong-min enters, he senses an immense shift. Yun-suk is nowhere to be found, but her outfit is folded on the bed. All the lights are off. The bed, dressers, and nightstand are unmoved, the hamper's overflowing clothes not a wrinkle different, the bathroom door hanging lopsided, per usual. But the room is entirely changed. It sounds moist. It glows.

—No. There's one new garment. It's crumpled on the floor, far from the hamper. Almost beneath Hyeong-min's boot toe. As he steps back, he kneels. The garment is a bodysuit the color of sepia chamomile. A molt? It's delicate and pliable. It's folded on itself like thick, wettened paper. Hyeong-min recognizes the beauty mark dotting its shoulder before he recognizes the vacant, sagging face, the paint brush-swipe of black hair, or the keratinous glimmer of nails.

A titanium ball peers out of the creased skin like a lone jewel. Cellulite swirls around it, ripples left from invisible waves. Hyeong-min touches the emptied breast it's attached to. It's warm.

"welcome home."

Yun-suk, Hyeong-min registers, is everywhere.

Every millimeter of the walls and ceiling are sunken in ticks. They cover the vents. They cover the windows. Because there are millions of them, they swallow any gaps or indents, leveling every surface in a rippling, rhinestone sea of arachnids. Their opalescence illuminates the room; their movement fills it with tidal noise.

"you look like you've seen a ghost!" Yun-suk frets from every crevice. "sit down, Hyeong-min! rest."

Will this, too, pass? Hyeong-min bursts into laughter. There's nothing else to do. He sits down heavily on the floor.

"What did you do?" he says. "You didn't hurt yourself, did you?"

"no, no. i unzipped myself."

When the ticks' legs fan out, they make black ripples, inverse of the way sunlight dapples moving water. Hyeong-min feels seasick. He closes his eyes to get his bearings.

"i love you."

"I know."

Although vulnerability bubbles at the edge of Yun-suk's many-faceted voice, Hyeong-min doesn't detect any desperation or hint of unhealed wounds. This is more extraordinary than anything. When he reopens his eyes and says "I love you too," tick-capped waves on the wall begin to lull, and their tide stops frothing at the floor. Yun-suk settles into a shining, placid, parasitic sea.

All is calm.

"You sound happy." Hyeong-min slips his shaking hands in his pockets. None of Yun-suk notices. She sighs dreamily. She has the same tone as when Hyeong-min has just finished inside her and they're entangled on the bed, indolent and mentally vacant.

"i am," she says. "i'm free! free, free, free!"

An iridescent, many-limbed whirlpool churns on the ceiling.

"you can't begin to know my relief, Hyeong-min. i'm not a woman. i'm ticks! i'm beholden to nothing!"

"I've tried to tell you that," Hyeong-min says, gently.

"you have. but you haven't borne my body. i needed to unshackle myself. oh, Hyeong-min, i've been a cruel liar to me, and you, and i was making a cruel inheritance for Seo-yun. no more. i can finally live as i please."

A waterfall of ticks cascades from the ceiling. It stretches towards the floor at a glacial pace, sparkling, seething. Hyeong-min, chin up, watches it descend on him.

"You aren't going to drink my blood, are you?"

He's half joking. He can picture the tick whirlpool exploding open onto him in a cut artery of longing; he can picture it unfolding onto him at a languid pace. There would be a greedy, tunneling tick head for his every pore and crevice. He would vanish under the abdomens ballooning with his blood like some bejeweled mummy.

Hyeong-min isn't sure he would run.

"no."

The tick waterfall nudges open a central slit in Yun-suk's bodysuit. It drips inside. The ticks coalesce into a not-quite-person-shaped pillar. Before Hyeong-min's eyes, their pearly appleseed bodies begin refilling the bodysuit into recognizable dimensions. They sound like the pouring of damp rice.

But even as her shape ripens in other places, the fingers don't finish refilling. Their tips hang limp. Yun-suk's face, too, refuses to fill—though it's regained volume, her features remain rubbery and dented. A dismayed wheeze escapes Yun-suk's lips. It reminds Hyeong-min of the gasp that escaped her when they had just begun dating, and he glimpsed her without makeup.

Of course. Returning to a familiar place is difficult, especially when you've fled. For all that he doesn't mind now, Hyeong-min eternally recalls the shame that suffocated him when he quit a job in tears, only for bills to insist he slither back and beg for reemployment three weeks later. Although two decades have passed, he knows the mortification of resuming a routine after being perceived.

"Hang on," he tells Yun-suk.

He takes her left hand and spreads her fingers across his. Her unfilled fingertips feel like silken gloves. Her pulse skitters over his. Slowly, a breath at a time, Yun-suk's hand develops. After it's finished, Hyeong-min can't tell it's made of ticks at all. He lays her finished hand across her abdomen before taking the other one. This one, too, re-renders itself.

Yun-suk looks at him. Most of her ticks have vanished inside her, but an anxious handful flicker around her nostrils and mouth in opaline snot trails. Her face remains cratered in the center. The last of its creases stick together like so many arms defensively folded over a bare chest.

"i'm afraid," she says. Hyeong-min can't tell if she fears the process or the end. The return.

"Don't be."

He cradles Yun-suk's head in his lap. He slips a thumb into her mouth, gently hooking the corner and pulling her open, saliva and soft, tick-covered tongue probing at him,

Yun-suk's fingers squeezing his wrist. They're hot. In the dark, the inside of her mouth shines, pebbled and titanium-bright.

"Seo-yun." Yun-suk is feeble and urgent.

Hyeong-min chews on the inside of his cheek and strokes Yun-suk's hair. He ignores the spike of pain in his forehead.

"Don't worry," he says. "We'll raise her no matter what she's made of."

Slowly, the last ticks ooze inside Yun-suk. They reassemble the veins and muscle strings. Slowly, Yun-suk's head inflates and unfurls, her features blooming. She's a moon revealing itself from behind trees. Then, finally, Yun-suk gives a shuddering breath, whole. Hyeong-min stares at the face cupped in his hands; the face stares back.

What can be said to a star? Hyeong-min holds the whole of Yun-suk, bright and quivering and many.

She holds him back.

galactic oracle eulogy

HEAR ME: IT IS THE SECOND CENCYCLE OF DECAY, the forty-fifth season of cancer, the third cycle of exodus from Indus the Magnificent, and I am the last oracle left.

For many eras, our peoples thrived in Indus: our titan, our world of worlds, our galaxy-cleaving vessel. We slept curled in aer cell clumps. We walked aer silk veins from aer skyrise heart to aer extremities—spacebitten digit-tips and arctic setae—to aer deepest wildernesses: the entrail labyrinths, the cerebral sea, the cloacal trenches. In our heyday, we venerated Indus daily for providing aemselves as cornucopia and citadel. Now Indus is dying.

I am too.

Though it's my duty to find and follow patterns, I feel little satisfaction in tracing Indus' long death parallel to my own. What pleasure is there in terminal empathy? As my body suffered, so did we: dermis colonies flooded inward as Indus' chitin cracked, and fleshrural dwellers fled as aer muscles quakecramped. Further exodus followed.

While my spawner was coaxing my larval self to stand, feeding their own stomach's worth of ironrich blood into my breastmaw, the marrow metropoli grew crowded with refugees who carried nothing but prayers. What else could they bring? Everything they owned was woven into their wasting homes.

Back then, my health was already deteriorating, but I was heavy with prophecy. This made me hysterical. Every ache was an omen, every counted breath and day part of an augury. My predecessors had encouraged endless excess. Our apocalypse felt inevitable.

Inevitable or not, it came. Vesselways closed beneath swelling tumors. Erratic breathing destabilized the lunglivers. Organplexes collapsed. Thousands clustered into thorax shelters as their homes squeezed into unlivable layers of pulp. The stomach peoples begged for assistance as Indus vomited all the planets aey devoured. Undigested rings and meteors crushed communities on their way up. Their children's entrails flecked the back of Indus' baleen alongside cancerous waste. For so long, they suffered. Today, they've been eaten away.

Yet since time is a body of beautiful, self-propelling loops soaked in past turns, the stomach peoples remain in my flickering visions, forever thriving, forever dying.

In a way, I tell (told) my spawner, *the cancer is an oracle. It knows growth is death.*

They gurgled in disgust.

Don't compare our blessing to that decimation again. My spawner knotted their shawl around my neckplace. *If you confuse blessings and curses, something will befall you. Mind yourself. We are different.*

A cycle later, they fled Indus on a globuleship without saying goodbye. I didn't know they were gone until someone neuronwired me the news. When I learned they'd abandoned Indus and me, some soft core within my chitin shattered. I couldn't even unravel this paradox. I laid inside Indus' aching heart. I ignored everyone's pleas. I cried.

Love, unlike cancer, has limits.

galactic oracle eulogy

* * *

When I crawl the organ centrals now, all is quiet. Dim. Their raw luster has faded. Membrane skies have turned muddy. Veiny constellations and landmarks have vanished, sickened, or shifted. The stretches of artery where whole neighborhoods would line up to suckle are empty. Waste clutters byways. I can travel for setalengths without sensing anyone. All the webs of stardust made meat, all our hopes stacked high in this homeplace alongside infrastructure and history, and it amounted to this.

Desolation.

If I swim the vesselways, I might find someone in a subcutane, but there's no guarantee the veins are open. So many are blocked by swelling tumors. The roads are already ruined from trapped commuters chewing holes in them to escape, even with saliva patches plastering those holes. I'm too weak to add to those injuries.

I crawl past wet ruin until exhaustion forces me to retreat.

* * *

It's fruitless, but I do my duties. I bathe in the aortal shrine's atrium until I'm cleansed. I chant, pray, and drink sacred blood until I'm sick in hopes it'll grant me the visions I once had. I try divining meanings from Indus' tremors. I perform pulse dances. Such rites used to be reserved for times of starvation. Now, they're routine. When I weaken, I unspool one of the fine vessels in the shrine, then latch it into my breastmaw. I feed. This rich blood is all that's sustaining me. When Indus goes, so will I. This leaves no room for hopelessness. My own undying tumors of acceptance and bitterness have forced it out.

I, too, am dying full of excess.

Oh, titan, tell me what to do. I stare at the three apertures above, watching them pump, alone, sore. *What ails you? How can you be hospiced?*

What hollow questions. Indus hasn't spoken since my grandspawner was oracle. I've divined needs through reading aer snot, cleansed aer heart, and directed our peoples to pull upon sinew and nerve to steer our titan through space, but I've never heard aer voice.

Perhaps aey're angry we neglected aem.

* * *

And still.

I sleep where my spawner and grandspawner slept. Eat where they ate. I stroke my shawl, tracing the pulsing web of fat, imagining what they would do, as if I don't know. While Indus and I rot in the consequences of my predecessors' choices, we live in all the cycles they loved us.

All that exists between swelling inevitability are apathy and abandonment. I stay with Indus less to prolong my life and more to enrich it: I'm dying a god's death, or aey're dying an orphan's, which has put oracle and titan closer than ever before. I am ending. So is our universe. It's all the same.

Hear me: it is the second cencycle of decay, the forty-fifth season of cancer, the third cycle of exodus. We are already gone, buried alive in our biotomb, but I pray that when Indus fleshcomets upon another galaxy, when the peoples of entropy eat our ruins, deduce meaning from Indus' cancer-chewed bones, and peer into the cosmos, they find no sign of us.

Only our unspoiled potential.

Only the stars.

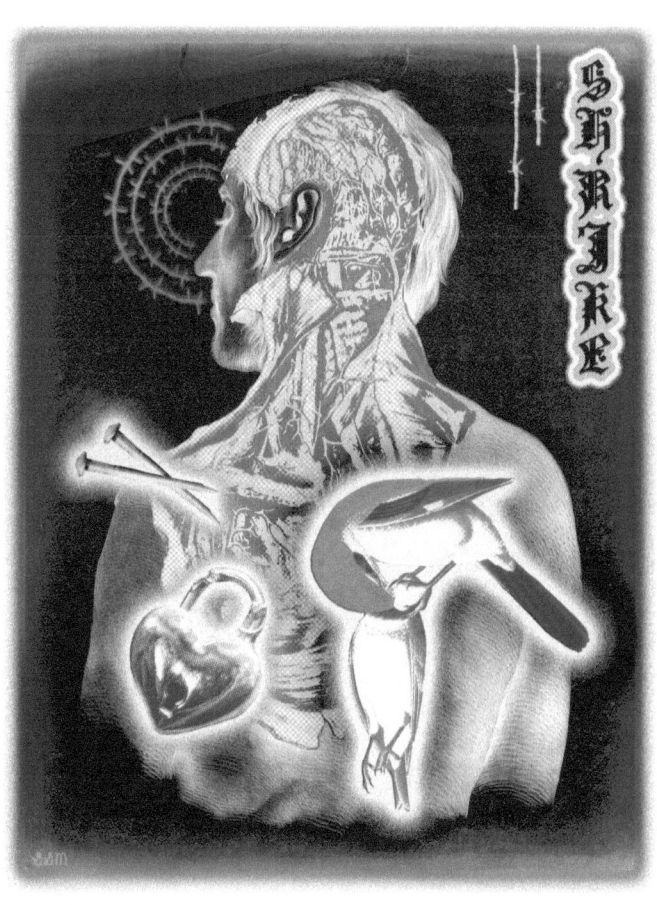

SHRIKE

The Tulane house has worn a hundred masks since its construction; before it dies—should it die—it will wear a hundred more. Long gone are the frat and its fifteen boys: all that remains of them is the sun-stenciled shape of an epsilon on Tulane's crumbling brow and the lewd, careless memorial plaques inside. Longer gone are the mistress who built Tulane and her servants that squeezed through its covert passages, worms in a palatial apple. Tulane is a bed and breakfast now, one that, until a few years ago, used to echo with paranormal investigators and tragedy tourists, but that too is fading. History oozes on.

Its threshold for titillation, too, changes. Once, a headline about thirteen fraternity boys getting flayed was juicy. Nowadays, it's prudish. The news discusses monsters liquidating sorority girls with acid, or debreasted flocks of cheerleaders strewn along highway gutters. Any story sans maggoty panty shot can't make it, Tulane included. So the house languishes now, a hostel barely breaking even, a brownstone labyrinth girdled by iron fences and oak branches.

As he walks up its driveway—his cane catching in the

cobbles, neglected briefcase hanging from one fist—#15 isn't sure Tulane has changed. He's wobbling without his crutches, so the world is tilted. Dead leaf heaps are swaying sands, the murder above cawing, judgmental smears on branch and shingle, porch jack-o-lanterns jeering, lolling heads. He pushes through the door that once knew him. It's harder than before. Those assurances murmured into his phone—just lies—come with an ease he finds disgusting.

Inside, #15 eats subpar eggs surrounded by a gallery of ghoulish halftone memories: frat photos, news clippings, crime scene sketches, autographed portraits of mid-tier ghost hunters. Above them hangs the mistress, immortalized in crumbling oil paint, jaundiced, a dark flower clutched to her breast. Orange and black crepe streamers crawl the space between frames, catching on curdling wallpaper. CRIPPLE LIVES, one tabloid headline screams; *he sure fucking does,* #15 mutters. His own Sprengeled shape takes less space on the wall than his symmetrical brothers but he derives a bitter thrill from seeing them preserved with haircuts and imposed golden attitudes they hated.

As he checks in, the receptionist asks, *Do I know you?*

No, #15 says, *not at all.*

* * *

titty posters, abandoned beer pong, cologne; secret doors propped open by bricks, disgust, radiator rumbling, uneasy jokes, time of numbers, new moon on window on wind-rattled branches on nail-scrape sound

who invited you in, quasimodo?—#14's fuckable mouth scowling; #15 hating him for it, for everything—*you did, asshole! you let me in this frat*

not me   the people that did are dead

voices tipping, tipsy hands slapping collar—*if you owned*

up to creeping we'd be cool—i'm not a creep!—slapping arm—*liar—touch me and i'll kill you—fine! get out!*

stumbling into house warren womb, shoe flooding with wet, tack piercing toe, angry, uncertain

don't spy on me again   #14 blocking cobwebbed door light closing it   hurt confusion dying in dark   breathing alone

breathing matched

* * *

The shirt stuffed into the left shoulder of his coat itches long before he receives his room key. The stairs are a struggle, always were, always will be; this house has long been hostile. #15 is hoping for his old room. He ends up with #14's instead. After he closes the blinds and undresses, his shoulder hungrily greeting the air, he shoves aside a chipped wardrobe. It's slow going. He's panting less than halfway through. #15 persists anyway. He knows what's behind the wardrobe. If he returned here on his dementia-ridden deathbed, he'd still remember Tulane's layout. His panting doesn't halt until the sounds of wood scraping do.

The door is unchanged: it's little more than a rectangle cut into the chestnut trim and curling floral wallpaper. If it wasn't for dust clumping in its gaps, or the tiny doorknob, it would look drawn on. #15 tries picking its lock with a bobby pin, then tries rattling it open. After that fails, he rests on the bed, overwhelmed by dead moths and the odor of cedar, studied by quaint ghoul, goblin, and cat masks. He leaves the wardrobe shoved aside.

When he can stand, he caresses #14's framed photo. MISSING! MYSTERY! the photocopied clippings shout.

You would've hated this. #15 presses his fingers into the

glass as if they can pass through that and time, as if he can gouge eyes or stroke skin. *And, again, I know: 'I told you so.'*

He ambles around until nightfall, counting obituaries, recalling chalk outlines of dismembered bodies, replaying memories in tacky, memorialized corners. He doesn't dare pull on false doorknobs or probe hidden passages. The sweat of anxiety beads his skin. What if someone recognizes him? What if there are questions? It's been two decades, yet this house's narrative still demands apologies.

Shut up, he tells the walls.

Crime scene negatives and the peepholes drilled beneath them don't reply.

* * *

bare bulb, autumn cold, mail stack; sweat between shoulders, chill between sweater threads, tension garroting temper   final, fleeting time before numbers

were you up last night?—#15 clutching undrunk coffee at the table, cautious; #14 pausing in paper ruffling—*no   actually, i was gone past seven   why?*—lips licked in silence—*i heard someone*

letters impaled on opener; flies pseudo impaled perching on photograph wall nails; half-lie impaled on tongue tip; phantom of gaze on neck

weird

* * *

At nightmorning's coldest, cruelest point, #15 is dreaming of a memory: loneliness, fraternal resentment, wrist beneath jockstrap waistband, another ball of nails outside his door, another beetle impaled at the center. An imprisoned gift-spectator to watch and be watched, a valentine given for performance. A suspicion: he shouldn't do this. A truth: this creates a secret. A reality: he touches himself for what watches anyway.

He awakens to a lock creaking. Wind shrieks at the house, trees, and weathervane. Ancient floorboards groan with weight. Shreds of orange moonlight thread them. The moonlight shakes, thrown from one spot to another by the oak's thrashing branches. #15 is rigid, his chest crushed by invisible pressure, his blood cold, skin hot, goosebumped. Rust creeps into his nose. None of the weight on him takes small, familiar shapes. It's broad and all-consuming. Suffocating.

Whatever watches from the jib doorway pretends to breathe. Its icy etching of a gaze is on him. #15 fights past his torpor and buried longings. He finds the name he learned in the dust of crawl space, broken plaster, and desire, but refused to say aloud. He claims it.

Shrike, he says.

Shattered moonlight flickers past the wardrobe.

#14's face floats in the opened door, unaged, smiling.

* * *

icy drizzle, ambulance tire tracks, bravado; beer bottles hurled onto false balcony, breaking glass, first ripe numbers picked, taste of iron behind gums, concept of company coming apart easier than body

i won't let them scare me! i fucking won't!—#14 raging on gravel drive, other eleven men watching, prickled with denial, eye-white terror—*you really gonna sleep in there?*—*yeah, pussy, i am! i'll die before i go home*—*that's not funny*—*you think i'm joking?*

sick, guilty elation, electricity between palms and gummy crutch grips, wrenching guts

they said it was all an accident

a choir of explosions—*are you stupid?—no way—what, do you want to believe someone did that?* silence

for #15, satisfaction

* * *

Have you been giving tours of the servant's quarters?

The receptionist folds his cash for next night's stay into the register. Her chipped purple nails shine in its empty gullet. *No sirree. Not anymore. They're too unsafe. We couldn't handle that liability. Everything's locked now.*

#15 nods. *Understandable.*

We've got a few treats though. Hang on.

She digs through a dented file cabinet. The stale candies on the counter stare from their bowl, a clump of acid-green eyeballs beneath translucent, crinkled lids. Dust wafts onto #15's sleeves when the receptionist drops a stack of aged museum labels before him.

If you're interested, she says, *you can have these.*

#15 browses the labels. There's one label about the servant quarters. The rest are all about Tulane's old mistress. Assumptions. A reprint of a portrait turned blurry by an archival game of telephone. Blurbs about her diary, her daily life, her occult leanings, her untimely death.

No thanks.

Your loss. The receptionist trashes the labels.

* * *

shattered wall, musty air, cobwebs; flashlight beams, bewilderment, mounds of melted candle, elbow dusted in plaster, stale ceremony, paranoia, sweat reek on ancient decay, crushed ambitions   five left

what is this?—those aprons and food jars are probably a

century old   the candles and blood, too—#14 and #15 pressing together to look into tiny revealed altar, #15's arm dripping blood onto #14's, canyon wall of melted wax, nails, and pattern in braided hair piercing their lights

no one's opened this for years

...i was so convinced we'd find its hideout   that i knew architecture   we're doomed—hey   it's not over yet—exhales overlapping, lips nearly catching, sudden step back, #15's shoulder slapped by swift retreat—*what the hell are you doing? —sorry   i thought—well, don't think anymore*

burning distance   #14 peering into the column of dark within the wall   both glimpsing an avian pendulum hanging from wire hangman's noose   #15 licking lips— *what is that?*

mummified flesh through gray feather patches, black hooked beak, white wing bars spinning in sacred, sacrificial illumination

it's a shrike

* * *

#15 sits on the porch, heavy, cane burning in his grip, a face burning in his mind. His thumb worries at the indent of an absent ring on his finger. Strings of paper bats bobble overhead. Nuthatches and chickadees scold them with a shower of moldy feeder seeds. This morning, too, is bright and cold.

When his arms aren't cramping, #15 draws every servants' passage he remembers on a napkin: three jib doors, the noxious coat closet of an interior corridor, the dumbwaiter, the claustrophobic stairs, the hidden altar, the crawlspace tunnels. Those condemned places the police swabbed for matter. He sketches this all with crayons found in his coat pocket. It's blasphemous to use them while alone. #15 does anyway. Although he trashes them when he's done, he slinks back to the garbage can immediately, fishes them out, and returns them to his coat pocket.

#14 had been the history major, the closeted architect, the one who'd pointed out that half their rooms were servant's quarters, and that after each night of exploring, those spaces were spiderwebbed with the brothers' spit and blood. He'd crowd visitors into the servant's passages at midnight, insistent on total darkness, urging them to rip from a bug-ridden apple bong—another party trick, a harvest season special—while smoking little himself.

Then he'd point his flashlight at the tally marks scratched into wood, and bandage linens hidden between boards, and say, *Did you know that the woman who built Tulane exclusively hired disfigured, illiterate girls as servants? She claimed it was charity. Would shame them into living in the walls. That's a secret this university keeps.*

#15 resentfully borrowed his knowledge then. He steals it now. All servant doors in Tulane lock from the outside. If their master key is sequestered in a drawer somewhere, rusting, chained in cobwebs, then either it isn't secured or locks don't matter.

He's long suspected they don't.

In the tar pits of his mind, he sketches #14's smile out of lightning and nails.

* * *

sloshing vodka, twilight, hammer under bed; bat cauldron spiraling outside, truce, backs against harsh metal bed frame, tailbone on hardwood, closing space between haggard numbers

sorry for what i called you last week   can't fucking handle being watched   not while all this is happening—bottle being passed, #14 and #15's knuckles knocking—*apology accepted you're still a bastard, but i get it   i can't comprehend all the dying—no, man, you don't get it—what don't i fucking get?*

pause heavy with windshriek and house moaning, harrowed face leaning in, overshoot, drunken mouth almost catching drunken mouth, alcoholic exhales merging

do you believe in ghosts?—i could, now

#14's throat bobbing   sheet crinkling behind back   *there was, is, one in my house   i grew up with it   every night, the fucking shower of stones on the roof   the gurgling   the constant, constant watching   the teeth   when i got older, it liked ... look, feel my hands*

fingers twining, calluses against scars and broken tendons, #15's intestines in knots—*jesus christ   how can you use them?* —shaking, gnarled fingers held aloft, nearly touching eyelash —*surgery   luck   i have fucking arthritis now, man, i just know i do   but i'd take this again over the watching   strange shit just finds me*

skin closer than shared futures that'll never come
strange shit has found all of us now

* * *

Are you from here?

The man who approaches after #15's phone call is young. He's armored in a gray, ghost-screen-printed shirt and serious demeanor. A video camera perches on his shoulder. It's angled towards him. He isn't concerned with the intensifying thunder overhead. When #15 pretends not to hear him, the cameraman speaks louder. Windchimes, loose boards, and branches rattle against the house, insistent, howling; he talks over them too.

No, #15 says, finally.

I'm a paranormal investigator. Agent 66. That's my

channel name too. He fiddles with his camera. *I'm here to investigate some lesser known phenomena at Tulane.*

Rain slaps the roof with the cadence of hurled sinkers and teeth. Whatever vibration #15 produces is enough: Agent 66 slides him two laminated photographs. One is of the false balcony.

The other, although old, is of him.

There's a growing theory, Agent 66 says, *that recent paranormal activity here isn't caused by the Flayed Fourteen. It comes from a hidden fatality: the fifteenth.* He taps the photographs. *Did you know that a decade after the tragedy, the handicapped survivor of the massacre returned to Tulane and committed suicide?*

Wow, #15 says.

'Wow' is right. He couldn't handle the guilt. He took his own life on this balcony.

#15 pictures the balcony now, a soaked, debris-whipped mess, a joke, an inaccessible flourish on a servants' room with brick-blocked windows and hingeless doors. He flashes to his third abandoned address staining the guest log. Many miles and moves stand between it and his regretfully permanent address. Reporters made sure of that.

Tulane has a mind of its own. Agent 66 has never ceased speaking.

Do you mistake automatons for people?

What? Agent 66 gestures at the thunder above.

I think the balcony's been bricked over.

Me too. Suspicious, isn't it? Agent 66 hums. *I think whatever netted the mistress a closed casket funeral still poisons this house. Look!* He points at the mistress' painting. *She's holding a talisman made of nails. It has ten points. Divide in half, and you've got five points. Her death aligned with Venus' orbit around Earth. The flower of Venus has a five point alignment. That's a pentagram she's holding, friend. Two of them.*

SHRIKE

Rain whips the windows. The house groans. If #15 squints, he can interpret the ugly flower petals as nails: sharp, shining, familiar.

I'm turning in, #15 says.

Agent 66 keeps whispering into his camera.

* * *

dead leaves, cigarettes, sunset; sunken, exhaustion-bagged eyes, untied sneakers on edge of concrete bench, rented tuxedos soiling around armpits, resignation, outline of cop car beneath oaks   cardboard in windows, ice packs wrapped around a shoulder and scarred fingers   countdown almost over

i'd rather die instead of dealing with this again—#14 sucking on unfiltered butt until cherry burns his lips—*you sure? i can't imagine being made a human jigsaw puzzle*—#15 ashing his own smoke, #14 spitting—*have you dealt with tabloid vultures? they dog you   overwrite you while you're alive   their fucking newspaper frankenstein of you replaces you, forever   that's real death   it got me as a kid   i won't choose that*

#15 twisting secrets and fears between his teeth   wire scars on inner thigh   uncertainty of dream or delusion   human anatomy map deep in gut filling, piece by piece

i want to live

#14 smiling in nicotine cloud, corners of mouth tearing

better you than me

* * *

He can't hear himself breathe over the storm that night, he can't see himself as human through the wild flashes of lightning and shape. #14's room is a tundra with no truth to it. As the jib door slowly opens, less a door than a widening void, none of that matters.

First, there's nothing. No one. #15, sheeted by cold, staring, sits in his bed, a phantom of the one he fantasized sleeping in or strangling in. Moments slip by in dark, slippery gasps: stones sliding from drowned mouth. Tulane rots.

Then, there's a triangle of cheek. A glint of teeth and glassy eye.

A beckoning finger.

#15 wobbles into the dark, naked except for his cane. It's enough. Barely. He pursues the vibration of footsteps into dusty, litter-knotted passages, torn crime scene tape and mouse shit and dead bat pups crunching underfoot. After a spell, vibration becomes delusion. He gropes his way through a place he used to know.

He turns a corner and collides with a body.

It isn't seamless. It isn't shaken. It rebounds against him like elastic, biting fence wire. #15's cane is torn from his grip. He shouts. A dusky, bare bulb flickers on. For the first time in over twenty five years, he is looking into #14's face.

Did you miss me?

#14's voice doesn't come from #14.

What stands before #15 is not a man, but many: fourteen shredded bodies collaged into one humming figure. White bicep smearing into olive forearm melting into black shoulders. Tan breast butting against brown ribcage against patchwork legs, buttocks, and pelvis. A crawling kaleidoscope of skin, body pieces of different dimensions sung and shoved together against their will. There must be organs within stolen from the first to go—the gutted—because #15's palm is sunk into a hot lower belly, the slipshod muscles and tendons radiant with unwanted life.

Because #15 hears flesh without voice or name screaming.

He stumbles back.

Return my cane, he says.

The Shrike smiles. It twirls the cane. Its lips are #14's lips; its hands are not. Volcanic judgment splashes through #15. He cuts it off before it can speak: *I'm not asking.*

House shudders. Bulb flickers. The Shrike's expression is flat, mortuary plastic. The many stale rings and draperies of dried blood on its skins flake. #15's vision tilts. Turns. His palms drip.

Alright, the Shrike says.

It sucks on the curve of the cane where the juncture of thumb and palm fit. It surrenders. #15 snatches the cane back. In the bulb's swaying illumination, the Shrike's mismatched patches of hair are crawling, curling illusions. Parasites or crosshatch made keratin. Metal glimmers in the gaps between its parts like phosphorescent marrow.

#15 recognizes its stained, shredded jockstrap as once being his.

I always knew I'd set this record straight, he says. *I always knew you were here.*

You left me anyway.

The cadence to #14's voice, singing with metallic static, has become sharper.

What, did you need *this head? You had other choices. You could've gained a voice sooner.* #15's knuckles clip unpolished wood; there is a soaring fury he hears as if it came from someone else. *You didn't take his hands. Were they too disfigured for you?*

Why are you speaking to me as if I'm him? Are you upset I had him first?

#15 massages the bridge of his nose. *No.*

His own trembling perturbs him. He's sparring with a ghost; he's attacking a fantasy. Truth watches from afar. He smells the Shrike, all sweat and ancient scab; its mockery of pulse wells against him with the sound of hail.

I've always liked you, the Shrike says, softly. The slink of curling wire emits from deep in its chest. *Watching you.*

Yeah.

I adored what you asked me to do.

#15 flushes in terror. *I never—*

Wishes called aloud in wet nightmares still count. There was a price to me. You believed everyone else deserved to pay it. Well, here I am. Here you are.

When the Shrike moves each of its parts ripples in the wake of a greater motion. It is blood in many neighboring cupped hands, or bone meal gelatin in lotus flower. A partitioned sea.

I can't stay forever, #15 says.

Why not?

My wife. My children.

Then stay now. They won't have to know. The Shrike's imitation of breathing crosses the distance between them heartbeats before its body does.

They don't.

The Shrike tilts its jaw and he sees it: the silver needling against its hair. The barren slit that splits its spine until the small of its back. Its vertebrae are brilliant, scorching snarls of barbed wire, saw blades and stars. They slice the air around them. Ruffles of unmet flesh undulate against them, sticking against them with one movement, parting the next.

Let me ruin you, the Shrike says.

A cruel, musty dream unfurls from where it slept in #15's head.

Please, he says.

He sets his cane aside. The Shrike grabs a fistful of his hair, holds him for just a second, almost tentative, before it shoves his face against the wall. The barbs that poke from between its mismatched wrists and hands—wire spikes bejeweled with rust and blood—bite #15's neck. The Shrike's mass presses on him. The smell of congealed scab drips into his squashed, open mouth. The fist in his hair grows tighter, tighter; it pulls him higher and tauter and his lips tear on splinters. He gasps. Fingernails pinch the skin between his shoulder blades. They break it.

I considered taking your head, the Shrike murmurs, a sting of pin and needle sensation on his earlobe. *I dreamed of your throat. Your voice as my voice. I wanted this more.*

Its fingers punch into him until they hit bone. He screams. Arches. Another inch of razor wire plunges into him. He's pliable. He's blood.

Stroke by stroke, the Shrike strips the flesh from his spine; his screams give way to moans as one seizing white pillar of pain after another blazes through him. There's a storm between his temples but he doesn't know if the downpour is rain or the explosion of blood from his body—on walls, on floor, on ceiling; he slips in it but the Shrike pulls him up by his hair. He sobs and calls for god. He's coming in half. *Cry,* it urges; a thick peel snaps. Cold air kisses #15's exposed spine. It's railroad tracks of pink bone flanked by shredded veils of fascia and twitching muscle.

He can barely stand in his own wet when the Shrike leans on the wall alongside him. It wraps his hand around a pulsing eel of his own flesh. #15 almost drops it: he isn't ready for the density of himself, its heartbeat, his own skin dressed in desperate fluid. The flesh strip's tail drags the floor, gathering bloodied dust, its rags of fat and membrane squirming. The Shrike's fingers squeeze between his until he grips it.

He seizes the Shrike's hair. His broken, throbbing nails catch scalp he always imagined clawing. It's colder than he imagined. More eager, less familiar. It isn't anything he knows. #14's voice splits with hunger instead of pained, hateful want. #15 almost breaks. He tries to let his vision die. To imagine both what he's receiving and what he always wanted. This mangling is victory.

He's still jetting blood, an explosion made man. When the Shrike braces itself against the wall he falls against it. Its wire vertebrae disappear into one of his hip gutters. It's so swift he can't register pain. Barbed wire pinches and crawls inside him; he sees its points rocking beneath his nearly split skin.

Complete me, the Shrike pleads.

He sinks his teeth into its collar to avoid screaming. He pastes the strip of himself between its shoulders. It sucks onto the barbed wire inch by squelching inch. The world quakes. Sloshes. He grips the tensing back that's both his and isn't, bruising it; he drinks the voice that isn't #14's as its cries leak between jabs of agony. It's far from home; it's better; it's neither. As he smoothes the last stretch of flesh onto the Shrike's spine, it bucks into him, hard; it crushes his hand against his pelvic wound. His insides run slick along his knuckles.

His red-webbed vision bursts into pure white.

* * *

crayons, goldfish crackers, dish soap   tiny sneaker pairs scattered on rug, schedules laden with shifts and grocery lists, patched drywall, comfort, resignation   pacifiers beneath spider plant pups   pink embroidered names   fragile mundanity

daddy i read a book about a ghost today—did you?—yes! it's important   they're real—across table, a dove's sigh, a wrist against silk bonnet, other against nursing baby's scalp—*she's definitely your kid—morbid stories are fine in moderation* fidgeting, tugging on skort pockets, missing tooth chatter maw

there was a boy who made friends with a ghost! it threw snowballs at his fence

a well opens

* * *

Past midnight, #15 awakens to a breast cradling his head.

His coat is stuffed into his flayed back. Fingertips trace his shoulder, a tongue only made warm by blood probing the split in his lips. In broken moonbeams, he sees the force that animates #14's eyes push them to smile. A necklace of blood-matted hair betrays where #14's collar meets wire and a rewritten body. The bed beneath them is #14's: the right one. Their presence on it is wrong.

Outside, wind flays the earth.

She'd cut their noses off in the courtyard, you know. The Shrike echoes #14 in its soft curiosity and condescension. *Put their eyes out with pokers. Clip their ears and lips with shears.* Sticky fingers walk along #15's hip. They hike the rim of his wound. *She loathed indiscrete servants. No point to the passages if guests saw them.*

Did they call and clothe you, or did the mistress force them into it?

The Shrike's smile is a rictus. A mistold joke. It rubs a blood-flaking thumb on his leg. *What does it matter? I made this body with you.*

#15 can't answer its question.

The Shrike gently slides him onto the comforter. Stands as he gasps and winces. Leaves. Turns in the stormdark doorway, one crimson splay of fingers on the wallpaper, a band of skin torn from its borrowed ring finger, its smile wide, teeth bright.

What do you think they'll decide about us, the Shrike says, *when we're both gone?*

#15 isn't sure it matters. In life, he continues: full of holes and false doors, doubling back on his own barbs even as he moves forward.

On paper, he's already dead.

dermestarium

Sergio is far too young to hear about the rot, but his father tells him about it anyway.

"It happened when I was in my mid twenties," Dad says, his speaker cranked to a nearly unbearable volume, his microphone bumping against the side of his fifteen-gallon jar, the maroon slush of him gently rocking inside it. "I was showering. Then suddenly, I thought, *I'm rotting*. And I was..."

Sergio picks at the lumpy birthmark under his breast. He nods, pretending to understand. Then his mother enters with the plastic feeding tube, funnel, and expired packet of applesauce, and wheels Dad's jar over to the sink for dinner.

* * *

Dad retells the story year after year, even as he liquifies further, even as his jars downsize, even as he and Sergio begin screaming at each other. His retellings double as Sergio begins growing mold. Yet in the end, it means little to Sergio. He awakens one day to realize he is thirty. Solid.

The window of terror has passed.

"How stupid," he tells himself in the mirror, eyeing all the grainy rings and splotchy hickeys of decay that carpet his body. "All those years crying on my birthday, and for what?"

Sergio is bathed in a bathroom fog of steam and cologne. It blurs the spotty rinds of green and lichenous haloes of black. He digs through a cabinet until he finds his lemon zester. He presses it to a crescent of black beading on his calf—one no bigger than a teacup setting stain—and angles the grater's teeth into his skin.

He nudges it forward. The rectangular mouths catch the mold. Several slivers of skin lift, like nails caught on the tips of bamboo skewers. Sergio pauses.

Something smells.

It must be an unwashed towel hanging behind him. Yes. That's been the answer for months. He withdraws the zester. Yanks a towel down. Lays it on the floor. Then Sergio takes the grater to his calf with a wet grind, sawing until it's cluttered with moist peels of skin, until the mold is gone, before starting on the next dark stain. Then the next. By the time he finishes, a blizzard of sludge cakes the towel.

Years ago, zesting like this would have reduced him to a broken, insomniac mess. Even more years ago, considering a zester or glimpsing a patch of mold would have sickened him. This annihilation is boring.

"At least it isn't worse," he says, as if his disgusting, raw circles can hear him. It's what he tells himself every day.

At least he isn't his father.

Sergio turns on the bathroom fan (he started doing this last year every time he grates), puts on more cologne (a habit established three years ago), rubs his mottled torso in deodorant (a tradition since last month), pulls on his clothes that don't squeeze too tight so his insides don't slosh, which he started doing two months ago, then applies more cologne—

god, he didn't know there were so many new routines; he refuses to look at them—and prepares for being perceived.

* * *

The day doesn't matter. Sergio melts through it. He clocks in. He works. He clocks out. He meets up with friends at a sushi bar. He smiles. He stares at the restaurant's aquarium. His friends inform the waiter it's his birthday. He lets a friend feed him sashimi even though it plunges down the chute of his throat into nothing. "I'm happy to be alive," he says, not even lying. His raw spots hurt. He lets a call from his father go to voicemail. He pours wine down his gullet even though it tastes like acetone. Everyone laughs.

Something smells.

* * *

Sergio gets home, feeling buzzed, and strips. Fumes of curiosity intoxicate him, but he isn't desperate. Not yet. He surveys his body in the funhouse strip of bathroom mirror, one foot cradled by a towel and damp skin-snow, the other stuck to cold linoleum. He's an expanse of brown dappled by barely veiled splotches of muscle. Rancidity shoved to the quick. If there's mold, it's present in constellations of green freckles. It's faint.

Sergio finds the puncture beneath his breast. His birthmark hides it. He probes the skin beneath the cherry angioma with his pinkie. It gives. His finger sinks into spongy flesh, then into a cavern. The stench of sweetening meat floods the bathroom. Sergio's lips purse. He hooks his pinkie around the puncture and rips it open. He works his ring finger in, then his other two. He tears, tears, tears.

Behind the whir of the bathroom fan rolls a thick splattering sound.

Sergio stares into the mirror, his urgency passed, calves and toes covered in reeking slush. It's warm. He sees only a cave rich with rot—fuzzy white, greens, shit browns, black, hematoma reds—and ribs curled around nothing, his fingers curled around them. His spine is a pillar, holding his head over the void. Steam wafts from his emptied torso.

'Come see,' he hears his father whisper. When Sergio reaches inside himself, his hands discover nothing. He's a chute with abandoned birthday food at the bottom. A pit grave. Sergio begins to cry before he imagines all his grief dripping into himself, moistening the cave.

He doubles over and screams into his clenched teeth.

* * *

This is his father's fault.

Why the fuck would a jar of slush have a child? Who let him have a child? He should've never reproduced. Dad's incomplete recollections of Sergio's grandmother vanishing while washing clothes, rinsed away by a current, never spoken of again, show that Dad had no parents. Not when it mattered. (This story was also shared with Sergio early. Childhood is a magic eye painting).

But there were siblings and cousins. There was Sergio's mother. *Surely someone was there to say, 'This is a bad idea,'* Sergio thinks, knowing there wasn't. His mother wanted a wall of blushing, breathing children between her and the military coups; his father was always more lonely than loved. Sergio imagines breaking his father's jar and pouring him down the drain, into a garbage disposal, into pipelines of refuse. Dad is no different from shit.

Shame sears Sergio.

dermestarium

What a horrible thing to think about the man whose greatest dream was to hold his son. Sergio claws at his legs in punishment. He flushes his rage-white dreams away. He stuffs another towel inside himself. Despite the fact that he did not beat the ruin, he sits at his dining room table in his usual chair with his usual coffee, sun slanting in on him in its usual way.

Sergio cannot decide if he finds this comforting or cruel. That's a conundrum he's used to.

"I'm losing," he says to himself, "but I'm not in last place. Dad was mush at my age."

Sergio plasters another tea towel against the barren expanse of himself. The fuzz has been wiped away, the slush gathered into the garbage disposal, the decomposition dried with pat after pat. The pain is always there. Sometimes he feels it. Other times, it just registers as his routine. He's too old for tantrums, but Sergio wants to throw himself onto the rug, kicking and wailing.

It's not fair that this is uneventful. It's not fair he can't look at what that means. It's not fair that tantrums were off limits to him as a child—tantrums, with a parent held together by glass? Unacceptable—to the point where Sergio now cannot tell the difference between expression and explosion.

"I'm going to fix this."

He tries to ignore the reedy quality of his voice. He cranks up a box fan pointed at the abyss of his chest, even as his skin breaks into goosebumps. He pulls his laptop over and places an order online.

When he's shivering too much to continue drying himself, Sergio throws away the single applesauce tub in his cupboard.

* * *

Sergio spends the next few days at work constantly checking his shirt buttons or excusing himself to refresh in the bathroom. All messages on his phone besides shipping updates mean nothing. He has to wait seventy-two hours for the package to arrive, and he slices the box open the instant it's delivered. The bedding-filled box also crawls with fuzzy black rinds: dermestid larvae.

Their casings and bedding smell of dry vomit. Sergio tips them into his tightening, drying torso. They patter in like rain.

"Eat," he commands. Begs.

Another feeble message from his father, garbled by voice-to-text, lights up his phone. The larvae are spreading static inside him.

They itch.

* * *

But dermestids only feed when conditions are right.

It takes time for Sergio to dry. He hastens the process by blow-drying his ribs every morning, careful not to blast any beetles. Whenever he can fit a flashlight or sunbeams into his chest, he stares at the hardening, shrinking inner lining of himself, tracking its changes. When he finds nothing he fabricates the change in his mind. He knows his skin-rot formations better than the backs of his hands, but this sinkhole within him is unknown. Its shifts all run together.

His friends worry about the persistent smell of vomit. Sergio dismisses them with the fact that he no longer drinks. He doesn't tell them it would be bad for the dermestids. He doesn't mention the dermestids at all, to them or his family. Yet they're unfolding: larvae overflow from him in dunes of frass and translucent shucked exoskeletons, trading their sooty, prickly shapes for shells, chewing his dry decay away with the precision of a craftsman dremeling latticework onto eggshell, ever faithfully eating and marrying in their dark world. Come spring, Sergio is thirteen pounds lighter.

dermestarium

When he looks into himself he sees the glow of dawn.

* * *

He calls his father one Wednesday evening after sweeping half the dermestid colony into a tank.

It's frosty, but crocuses are sprouting from the snow, purple pupae about to bloom. Sergio has a pyramid of hand warmers weighing his gut to warm the beetles. They crawl over his ribs and tightly buttoned flannel. When he picks up his phone, his fingertips sting with the cold. There's no moisture inside him to freeze. Sergio calls his father, kicks at chunks of slush, and waits for an answer. Five rings in, he gets one.

"Yes, hello?"

His father's voice is feeble. It echoes back in an attempt to convince itself it exists. The last time they spoke, Sergio's mother—married to his father on paper alone—told Sergio that his father was in a spaghetti sauce jar now, and only eating a few tablespoons of applesauce per day.

"Hello, papá," Sergio says.

"Sergio! Finally, you call. It's been weeks. I worried."

Sergio stares at the crocuses so he doesn't focus on the sound of tears dripping from the jar lid back into his father's mass.

They've called many times before now, but sat near silent on the phone each time. The preamble here is an unimportant collection of words about work, weekends, and errands. Sergio's palms turn sweaty and his dermestids churn as they approach what matters.

"Papá," he says, "I started rotting. Actually rotting."

"Oh," his father says.

The helplessness of it hurts and angers Sergio more than he expected.

"Don't worry," Sergio says, killing the apology he senses coming. "I'm dealing with it. I'm fine."

Now more than ever, it is easy to picture a little boy in another country learning his parent has melted into a river—no jar to catch them, no one to feed them—without knowing what's happened, or that this is his future. How easy it would be for that boy to decide on parenthood in his bid to right an incorrect wrong.

"How can you be fine?" his father says. "How? You are suffering!"

"Papá, cut it out."

"I did not want this for you."

"I know." Sergio tightens his grip on his phone. "Papá, be honest with me. Did you think about this at all before you had me?"

He hears the crawling of himself in the silence.

"No. I have thought about it since. Sergiosito, do not take this the wrong way—"

"I won't."

There are ducks overhead. Sunlight on the snow. Beetle-stench in his sinuses.

"I love you," his father's garbled voice says, "more than anything in the world. I shouldn't have ever had you."

Sergio stands alone on the sidewalk, a larva crawling out of his nose. The relief comes as a monsoon.

"That's all I've ever wanted to hear," he says.

Twilight Tide

THE REDFISH IS REMARKABLE BECAUSE DESPITE THE fact it's dead, it is still moving. Opal, straw flip-flops in hand, watches it arrive. The dimmed, bloated body (once golden, once maroon) pushes itself onto the beach. With one tail sweep after another, it lurches past mangrove roots and driftwood. It stops once it's struggled above the tideline.

Opal approaches once it flops over. The redfish's milky eyes bulge at her. Seaweed snarls its fins. Its missing scales resemble gray, naked nail beds. Opal clutches her sunhat and covers her nose when the wind casts salt into her face.

She is about to ask the redfish what it wants, since nothing dead needs anything, when it clenches its distended stomach. The redfish's powerful, hook-punched lips give way to dark matter. It retches silt onto the white sand. Sediment from the bottom of the bay fans from its mouth. It's a horrible mixture, rich with distilled death, softer than slime. Opal screams when she spots the wedding ring half-buried in it.

She bolts to the fish and kneels in its putrid wake. Opal snatches the wedding ring from the slime. Sundress forgotten, she smashes the ring against her chest to clean it. Umber rot stains the linen. Opal turns the ring in her hands until she almost drops it, then slides it onto a shaking finger. The silver band fits as it always has.

Opal, on her hands and knees, looms over the fish. Her hair dangles around her face like an unraveling net. Above, egrets soar.

"Where is he?" she says.

The redfish doesn't respond. Opal seizes its fin, her fingers sinking into the soft bloat, and rolls it onto its side. She leans in until its soon-to-stink body tangles in her curtain of hair and her lips almost snag on its spiny teeth. Garbled, unfinished noises burst from Opal. The redfish's gills threaten to slice her cheek.

"*Where is he?*" she says. "Tell me. Tell me."

No answer comes. The messenger, having delivered its message, disintegrates into rotten chunks. Opal shakes the fish carcass several more times before apologizing. Then she sits in her pooled sundress, the lacy froth of incoming tide eating at her legs, fingers clenched in a white-hot grip around her ring, and stares at Bon Secour Bay.

The sunset she came to see washes over the water in smears of dreamsicle and blood. The sun, a blinding dot, lowers itself into the gulf. Wind tassels the cypresses. Crabs emerge to clean the dead. Pelican-shapes slash the fading sky. Opal, rocking, hands juddering, mouth spitting fragmented words, doesn't care about any of it. What she longs to see are the depths.

She stays on the beach even as mosquitos puncture her skin and darkness swallows the shore.

* * *

It's difficult for Opal to explain anything to anyone. She is too forward. Too clear. It's impossible for her to explain that her husband who walked into the sea a decade ago, who she loves (and loathed) more than anyone in the world, has reached out to her.

She still tries. Despite what others think of Opal, she isn't immune to elation, or the urge to share good news.

"My estranged husband spoke to me," she says, while fishing for cash in her wallet. "We're trying to reconcile. It's all I can think about."

The bait shop clerk, a grizzled butch, stares. She frowns when Opal flashes her wedding ring. They're surrounded by a claustrophobic labyrinth of tubes, tanks, and marine creatures, but the butch looks at Opal as if she's the most offensive entity present. Opal (forced to wear earplugs so the crosstalk of tank filters and people doesn't render her rabid) still takes offense to that.

"Opal, honey, ain't he dead?"

The butch makes 'honey' into a seawall. A pseudo-friendly way of keeping Opal at a distance. It took Opal years to clock this. She no longer cares. At least the butch is honest. Opal shakes her head. For the hundredth time, she rotates the ring to bloodlet her jitters.

"No," she says. "Itai isn't dead."

Drowning isn't consensual. Opal knows that her husband let the seawater into his lungs in an entirely different way. Technicalities are important. She isn't sure what's become of him, but she's never doubted that he's alive.

The butch makes an unconvinced noise. She takes the ten from Opal's fingers to make change. The bag of shrimp Opal bought slumps on the counter. The shrimp glide around their prison, legs curling, their blue cores pulsing in their own translucent cages.

"Even if he wasn't dead," the butch says, "I'd be afraid to ask why you're excited to see a man who ain't done shit for you in a decade."

"He's a good partner," Opal says. "He supports me."

"How?"

Despite the openness of 'how?' it isn't an open question. People never want an exhaustive explanation. At worst, when given one, they assume aggression. At best, they feign interest while projecting martyrization to everyone else. Opal never sensed that. Someone told her that while attacking her. It was a valuable lesson.

She's never forgotten the humiliation.

Opal says, "Itai always pays his part of utilities."

"Ain't you been paying that with his life insurance payout?" the butch says.

"As I said, he pays his part of the utilities." Opal thrusts the bait bag into her tote.

The butch retreats behind the counter. The tourists in the bait shop, clustered around the tanks and the corkboard full of 'missing' posters, murmur to each other. Maybe some are local. Opal cares so little that she recognizes none of them. They are beneath shrimp. She at least understands shrimp.

"Enjoy your day, Miss Opal," the butch says.

"It's Mrs."

The butch retreats further at her loud, flat correction. Someone clears their throat. Everyone makes way for Opal as she exits, though they aren't near her.

She's seen schools of fish do the same for sharks.

* * *

"I hope shrimp is still your favorite," Opal tells the black waves. "I hope they get to you. I hope you weren't sending the ring to divorce. I still want you. I've never hated you. There's a difference between your presence and you. I can explain that now."

The boat ramp concrete gnaws at her soles. Algae slicks

her skin; fish hook and fish bones prick her toes. A shroud of Spanish moss whispers behind her. All the picnic tables in the park are empty. Opal only came here after the new summer renters called the police on her (she's always groundskeeping or trespassing on her own property) but she's grateful for the privacy.

"It's hard to exist." She fiddles with the shrimp bag. "You understand that, don't you, Itai? Sometimes I'd feel you in bed next to me, not even touching me, and it was like hearing the electric in the walls or feeling grocery store lights. It was unbearable. I hated it so much I couldn't sleep. You were like some boiling black hole put next to me to torture me.

"But I couldn't ask for space. I didn't know how to. We didn't *have* it, not in our house. We still don't. And I was terrified that if I left, or asked you to leave, you'd think I didn't love you. So I laid there wishing you'd just fucking die."

Far out in the bay, beneath the singular moonbeam spotlighting the water, something razor-shaped breaks the surface. Maybe it's a wave. Maybe. Opal restrains herself from crying out. From trying to swim to it.

"I never wanted that. I never meant anything I said while being alive made me insane. It still does that, but I deal with it now. Mostly." She speaks faster when she senses her voice failing. "You're the only person I've ever missed. Everyone was right about me being a monster. But I do love you."

The razor crest in the waves is gone. Opal's voice vanishes. Her sob thrashes inside her body. She releases the shrimp.

They vanish into the gloom.

* * *

It's unfair, Opal knows, that she's counting the seconds since she released the shrimp. That she's counting the minutes. The days. It's unfair that her words are bad. It's unfair that for years, she blamed Itai for their separation, then blamed herself. It was both of them. It's always been the both of them. Neither of them have ever stepped foot in a store, a school, or a doctor's office (or a family gathering, before their families finished dying) without being unwelcome. They're together in everything, even separate.

Did you hear? Another boat sank.

"You weren't easy to live with," she tells her reflection. "I want to try again anyway." She repeats it into Itai's wool sweater she sleeps with, then his sparsely decorated corner of the room. There's nothing else to repeat it to. Her husband didn't leave much behind. He possessed little besides himself.

The one constant besides that was Itai's unease with his own body. Even after the injections, after the filet scars that reshaped his pectorals and pelvis, he remained lost. Opal had resented the way he'd floated in their lives, as if he was a jellyfish overflowing from a tiny tide pool while the water ebbed away.

Nah. No one died. A shrimp boat picked them up. But they said...

Every few months, Itai would shrink. He'd beg Opal for her clothes, then clung to them, to her, before ranting about how hideous he was. He never recognized their shared bay of a body. The concept that his words poisoned them both was unfathomable. Then when he was done gutting himself, when he was done injuring Opal, he'd swell.

Opal misses her husband now, not just the concept of him. She doesn't miss the pounds of seafood that cycled through their refrigerator. The parade of baggy clothes that washed through the house before Itai starved himself down, trashed them, then started anew.

I dunno. There's something strange.

Perhaps he's found peace in the gulf. He must have. When their marriage became a slipped disc, when agony displaced something soft, they had agreed to separate until they both changed. Opal, afraid of her edges, chose land. Itai walked himself and their rings into the oncoming surf.

Hopefully, his metamorphosis has been good. Hopefully, they'll speak soon. Hopefully, their changes haven't made them hostile to each other. With the renters gone, Opal walks circles around their house's stilts to avoid considering the worst. Her gray streak doesn't need to widen. She needs no more personal or historical loss.

Something's in the water.

She spends every night dreaming of bioluminescent stars in a bleak, wet sky.

* * *

Six days, eight hours, and thirty minutes after Opal sends her gift, a surprise arrives alongside the news of two sunken sailboats and one missing person: a crevalle jack.

Opal almost trips on it when she steps out to water her banana tree. It's massive. Four feet of silver, emerald, and ochre. Seventy pounds of forked-fin generosity. It has rolled itself up to her stairs. Flies clump around the bite taken from its stomach. The hook that dragged it to an exhausted death shines in its nostril. Its shredded intestines haven't yet lost their color.

When Opal gasps, its eye rolls to look at her.

Opal keeps her ring on while she butchers the jack. She periodically stops to link her fingers and clap in excitement, even when she's slick with gore. The sticky knell of her palms is a chime of gratitude. It floats over the hissing waves.

She buries the bones at the foot of her banana tree. After dinner, she releases a tiny paper plate of fish onto the water.

It floats out of sight.

* * *

For every torn trawling net, capsized boat, and uneasy story from an oilman, there is a gift from Itai: an endangered slaughtered sawfish, an eviscerated ochre-and-silver pompano, a fistful of ballyhoo dropped into the wrong waters, a young bull shark heavy with lead, a delicate, deepsea stranger destroyed by a change in pressure. All the refugees killed for a heavenly yacht fleet's feast crawl, slither, and flop their way to Opal's feet.

A hand washed up on the beach.

Time means nothing outside of deadlines or paychecks. After a stillborn dolphin gets caught on a crab trap line for days, unable to reach Opal until it's eaten to the bone (something she broods about even now) she ceases waiting on the beach. She waits in the shallows.

An abandoned trawler drifted ashore.

As a guilty pleasure, as a precaution, she begins going to the park. For a week, she sits breast-deep in boat ramp water every night, salt licking her chin, stingrays gliding around her, undead vow renewals swimming into her lap. (So does litter. She pushes that away).

The crew left it in lifeboats.

"Do you finally feel comfortable?" Opal strokes the underbelly of the flounder blanketing her lap. Gigging punctures speckle its gut. "Can I trust you not to hurt me? Be honest."

Bon Secour Bay is shallow. She could walk for miles without swimming. Opal fears how she'd look by the time she reached Itai. Her brilliant, ripping terror is gone, but trepidation remains.

We can't divulge the details...

The flounder gently mouths her fingers. Its serrated teeth don't scratch her. Opal's reverie shatters when some drunk teenagers, fearing for her safety and sanity, begin yelling at her. Then, when they recognize her, the bottle hurling starts.

She walks home full of glass and apprehension.

* * *

Opal isn't sure who's giving in return to what.

Her banana tree's leaves swell into veiny, carnivorous hearts larger than her head. Hope tears at Opal as much as fear. It's rawer than honeymoon love; it's more ragged than gull-torn entrails. In her extended isolation, she forgot the feeling of company. To be tempted with it awakens her from hibernation. It sets her insides churning.

Opal starves. She can't go out without loathing the faceless shunners around her or grasping for them. An atrophied need for community clashes with her exile. How did she last so long without Itai? How can she ensure this hunger doesn't rush her decision? All of her attempts at conversation get regarded as rude; her 'hello's receive discomfort. Her scabbing wounds provoke unease.

Something's living under the rigs.

The safest landlocked entity in her life is the bait shop butch. Another outcast. Opal claws her way into check-out conversations whenever possible. She can tell the butch is uncomfortable. She's too desperate to care. One Saturday, she laughs at the news that a trophy fisherman fell onto his own propeller and died. The butch drops Opal's uncounted cash.

"What the hell is wrong with you?" she says. "Someone got hurt! Someone died! How is that funny?"

Opal thinks: 'why isn't it funny that the tourists are scared? Their grandparents hunted mine. They're trying to price me out of my inherited home. They're trying to hurt my husband. They scream into the sea. They slice manatees. They drag fish to death for sport. They spread disease. Isn't this funny because it's deserved? Isn't it nice to see someone else be the raw nerve?'

Opal says: "It just is."

I reckon it's a monster.

The butch asks her to leave.

* * *

"Do you still think I'm tender? Do you think I'd stay that way if I joined you?"

Opal speaks to her reflection in the glassy water. Miles away, on the bay's otherworldly rim, oil rigs smoke. Dawn hasn't broken. The oncoming storm hasn't arrived. Copper stings Opal's gums.

She would rake her palm across sharpened barnacles for someone in need. She shoos cottonmouths across the road. She is capable of joy; of pleasure. Does it matter that she (apparently) has the eyes of a shark? Why is she inhuman for hating people that harassed her and her husband? Why must she smile for outsiders destroying a bay they don't think she deserves?

Must she bleed and cry in public to show she feels?

That wouldn't move the shambling shoals that live here. They would see it as an illusion. While apart from Itai, Opal has learned there is no proving herself. This world is simple: if enough people deem something true, it is. Belief trumps reality. Her peacefulness means nothing. Itai's softness meant nothing. The idea of their violent potential equals action.

The majority has spoken: her husband was wrong about her humanity.

So Opal is a predator. She is a cold, clockwork beast made for evil. Her bones are cartilage, her skin sandpaper, her teeth ever-replenishing. If regret or guilt ever dragged her backwards, they'd flood her gills and kill her. She is thus incapable of these emotions. Might also be incapable of pain.

What do sharks feel when sliced open? Probably little.

Probably nothing.

Only one person believes in Opal's vulnerability (has laughed with her, consoled her, and pleased her, when she could stand touch) and he's been underwater for a decade. Who knows what discoveries Itai's made in the murk. In the labyrinth of oil rig legs or sunless open sea.

It's hard to tell exactly what he wants when he isn't here. He may not believe in her anymore. He may not even be a person anymore. Opal only claps in anxiety when she considers the former. The latter might bring them closer.

"Itai," she says, before her voice flees, "I need a sign you trust me."

She spits into the shallows.

Minnows eat her saliva away.

* * *

An evening later, the next gift comes from deep water wrecks.

The snapper is nothing but scaly muscle rolled in a red-to-coral flush. Its eyes are scarlet. It's small, this gift slain out of season, but it crawls its way up the shore on tattered fins and tenacity before Opal can see it. When she takes it into her hands, it opens.

In the prickly keepsake vault of its mouth sits an isopod.

It stares at Opal. She stares at it. The isopod, as if to greet her, begins waving its legs. It's a terrible, flesh-fed gem. It glitters. So does the object in its grip. Opal's heart overflows in its presence. She reaches for it. With legs crafted for killing tongue, the isopod offers her a rusty heart-shaped locket.

Inside is a molar and a patch of shining, slimy skin.

* * *

Opal drives twenty minutes to Gulf Shores, a paradise of palms and bulldozed dunes, to test her taste for humanity. She enters a tourist trap across from gated beachfront property: a cornucopia of towels, neon inflatables, and bottled fetal sharks. Earplug-less, she faces the vacationing crowd. A century ago, Opal's people tended to this shore. That knowledge sits in her stomach with the swallowed locket.

With every wave of noise the throngs blend into doughy, gaping tides: storm surges carrying pounds of plastic, wealth, and desecrated dead. This is no graveyard of gifts. It's an abattoir of cleaned, price-tagged victims. Is this worth staying landlocked for? A woman side-eyes her.

They remove Opal when she starts screaming.

* * *

The storm is meant for them.

Not intentionally. Opal and Itai have always accommodated forces meant to destroy them. While everyone else ties down their catamarans then flees for condos on calmer shores, Opal sits in front of her rotting bulkhead. She stays put as rain stings her face. It soaks Itai's sweater, then her otherwise naked body. Seabirds flee the yellow sky. Opal, eyes closed, lets saltwater lick its way up her calves.

The gifts arrive with the darkening sky: anglerfish with lovers fused to their sides, decapitated sailcats heavy with roe, pebbles from ruined fish nests. A celebration of change. Carnal grotesqueness. Opal's fingers dip inside her. Her moans lodge in every coil of shell and empty segment of crab claw, ready to empty themselves into the depths when they wash out.

Opal keeps fucking herself even as pieces of ruined homes

wash ashore. Even as driftwood hurls against her shins, bruising her. Milky froth washes in on the waves. It spikes in and out with the tide. It sprays between her curled fingers, eager to enter her. She feels the gifts, soft and skin-like, crowd her thighs. They hickey her hips. A roaring wave builds in Opal's ears as the tide recedes. She digs her teeth into her lip and arcs her body towards the oncoming storm. Her nerves scream, begging for destruction.

The wave makes land.

Seawater shoots into her nose, into her eyes, into her; a stray paddle turned javelin collides with her jaw. Her teeth slam shut on her lip then through it. Opal's nerves explode. When the wave withdraws, Opal, all of her ringing, elbows on the sand, holds blood and creamy milt in her mouth. Her neighbor's skiff, tether broken, floats nearby. Her lungs burn: not for the lack of air, but the excess of it.

The gift begins dripping out of the hole below her lip. It burns. Did Itai's first gulp of bay feel like this? Opal swallows. Her old fears vanish. Sandy hair and palm fronds catch in her wounds. Itai's sweater squeezes her. She is ice water, hot current, and agony. She is alive.

She understands what her husband saw in the bay.

"Alright, Itai," she rasps into the surf. "I'm ready to try again."

Opal sets out for the oil rigs. The skiff bounces across waves so steep she fears they'll break her in half. Her bones throb. The bay fumes. By the time she reaches the first oil rig, stormdark engulfs her. Only flare stacks and the scarlet pulse of rig lights pierce it. Curtains of lost bobbers and fishing line debris drape from their pilings. A hanged tern rots in one. She cannot see past the wind or pelting rain.

All quiets.

The engine dies.

Opal, nerves still aflame, hears herself panting. The water is dead. Black. There is no difference between the sky and the depths. The storm circles her, raging, pacing. Opal glides between oil-sucking monoliths on the last of her momentum.

"Itai?"

It's been so long. Staring into the unknown is worse when she used to know it. Opal isn't here to wound; she's too old to survive wounding. She aches. She waits, turning her ring.

A constellation lights beneath the boat.

Itai rises from the deep at a glacial pace. Even then, his ascent rocks the boat. He's longer than it by several feet. Sparkling lateral lines trace his sides. A long, maroon fin trims his serpentine form. He is quicksilver married to molten glass. A man blown into an oarfish. As his plumed head breaks the surface, Opal recognizes the remains of a human skull under his skin. When his vestigial limbs grip the edge of the boat, metacarpals glitter inside them, outshone only by a band of silver.

Extra bones streak Itai's body alongside bioluminescence. A wavy rib there. A thread of radius here. The debris of humanity. He's been smeared into a deepsea comet.

The boat groans. Opal rushes to the other side so Itai can heave himself in without tipping it. His coils land in the bottom with a crash. The boat sinks, its rim almost even with the surface, as all of Itai piles in. His eyes are quicksilver discs the size of her fists. Nothing reflects in them but iridescence.

Opal unfreezes when she realizes Itai is uncertain if she can bear being touched.

She opens her arms. A whole sea's worth of coils piles into them. The boat overflows. Sinks. That doesn't matter: her teeth are against teeth, her hopes against hopes, her sticky flesh against sticky flesh. Opal's desire for sand and sunlight extinguishes when her husband's depth-distorted voice speaks her name.

She imagines quiet twilight waters. She imagines a place meant for monsters, and gliding alongside company forever.

She imagines being able to bite.

i've missed you, Itai says, the taste of the drowned on his breath. *every day.*

Opal opens her mouth for him and the gulf.

entrada

BEFORE GOING FURTHER, YOU ASK THE REAL WOMAN if she's sure of herself. She halts, a hand on your fly, and gives you a reproachful look. Even in the dim closet you wither.

of course i am, she says. *why wouldn't i be?*

Her nails scrape your belly. You lick your lips. You're jackknifed into each other in this coat closet, one of your knees against the accordion door, the other against wallpaper, the real woman between them. Hat boxes and boots pile against you; coats hang above in a suffocating smog of cedar and fur. Chatter echoes through the worm-eaten walls.

sorry. most people don't know how to handle me.

You've been apologizing since birth. It's instinctual. The obstetrician was glowering at the clusterfuck below your hips before anyone wiped the vernix from your body. No amount of forced and consensual transitions have made your maze more parsable. Your teeth grind together when the real woman unbuttons your pants.

you doubting me is a real unplug, she says.

i know. i just wasn't sure...

The real woman's skirt is inside-out. A tag dangles from

her waist like a tiered tongue. Her bra is on so tight it sinks into the space between ribs. If it tightens any more, her torso will pinch off and float into the coats.

i'm not unpunctured, she says. *i've slept with plenty of strange people.*

Shame and reassurance radiate from where her fingertips touch your lower stomach. Perhaps she *will* know what to do once her touch gets lower. Nausea throbs up your core alongside arousal. You open your mouth to apologize again when she opens you: her fingers curl into a rigid scoop and sink through your treasure trail.

Through your skin.

No.

Not again.

You gasp as manicured nails squirm into you. The hand weaves through the loom of flesh above your pubis. It twangs countless threads of muscle on the way in.

i know what sex is, the real woman says, unfazed by your writhing. *it's entry.*

A glint of defiance cuts her voice. It's as if she found your question condescending. She wriggles her fingers into the crevice between abdominal muscles. Shoves. There's a pop. Her wrist vanishes inside you. Your vision narrows to a blurry pinprick. Cold sweat drips between your legs. Her hand rips the same reaction from your body that a badly placed needle during a blood draw does. 'Vasovagal' is the most sensual, rancid word alive.

The real woman continues to talk about sex as if she's reading an engine manual. She uses a seductive voice, but it's the halting drone that comes from a popper-decimated pornstar in pigtails reading an offscreen script: a performance in the right key for everyone but you. The difference is that you flinch when tools puncture that pornstar's gummy stomach and she squeals.

entrada

The difference is who's violated.

You begin wheezing when the real woman's forearm rubs against your navel. Blood and fat lube her arm. She is so close she's almost tonguing your exhalations, but her lips are pursed in concentration, her brows needled together at a fine point. When your mouths brush it is no kiss. You don't cry. If you cry, the guilty confusion and anger arrives.

A hand grips your pelvic bone.

god! You retch words so vomit doesn't spray out. *god! god!*

The real woman bares her teeth at you in what must be a smile. Judgment flickers through her gaze.

what a pretty parrot you are, she says.

Your hips convulse as her palm crawls over your pubis. It squishes into your depths. Hat boxes clatter. In your triple-vision, you see a prolapsed slit of muscle contracted around the real woman's arm, forming the hole you've never had.

It's weeping.

The real woman's smile fades when her fingers knock against your sacrum again. Your ligaments floss her skin. Laughter seeps in from the living room. You need its presence to force you through this.

hang on, the real woman says. *i'm almost to the holespace. but our angle is bad.*

The threat of novelty horrifies you. No one has ever sunk past the upper pelvis. What holespace can she mean besides the one she's made?

what do you mean? wait. wait.

The arm breaks inside you.

You feel the wrist go crooked. The snap reverbs up your spine. Bone rakes your innards. The real woman grunts. Pushes. Then there's a hand in the crooked, unformed cavities doctors have only discussed in numerical scales, scans, and terms of treatment, and fingers plucking at the unknown as if they're lute strings.

you see? She says. *easy.*

Fluid weeps out of you at every possible lower aperture. You choke on yourself when the snapped wrist rocks back and forth. Nails finger your shredded internal secrets. Contractions of terror spike through you.

i'm blacking out. You claw into the hardwood. *please—*
good boygirl. good hole.

You bite into the lower hem of a fur coat to scream so no one hears you. There's no way out besides finishing. Your pelvis thrusts in an attempt to dislodge the intruder inside it until your consciousness gives. You dissolve into fragmented soup. When you awaken, the shattered hand is unfucking its way out of you. Bone catches your skinpeel the way teeth catch lip.

You collapse. The fingers squelch free. All is dim, all is static, but you sense that the real woman's hand drips with you. You lay there, a scrap between scraps, at least two nails broken off between floorboards, while the real woman massages herself back into shape. The house, another receptacle, spits fragments of conversation onto your unbuttoned body.

my turn. The real woman sucks on her wet fingers so hard that you hear skin break. She shoves them back to their knuckles, flutters her eyelashes at you, and hikes her skirt.

i can't. You slam a heel on the skirt hem before she reveals the nothingness you know is beneath. *sorry.* You cradle your pulsating, closing fuckwound. It weeps against your palm.

There is glass inside you. Between your legs. In your skull. In your torn-untorn wrong places. You always hope this hurts less. It never does. The real woman scowls.

fine. She huffs. *i thought you'd care about mutual unmakery. but. whatever!*

It sounds like an attempt to convince herself she knows pain as more than a feeling she's shared a room with. The real

entrada

woman stands. She presses against the accordion door while you breathe raggedly, tuck your shirt in, and zip your pants. Your belt loops are moist. The longing to limp to your room, cup what's between your legs, and sob overwhelms you. You'll never know yourself more than strangers' hands or surgeries do.

Maybe this is punishment for trying to.

You claw yourself up the closet wall to stand. Before she opens the door, the real woman looks at you, threads of light stitching her silhouette. She's pretty. Solid. So sure of her own existence that if a doctor diagnosed her with any incorrectness, she would declare *no!,* and they would disintegrate. When she straightens her clothes, it's with a diet version of insecurity. It's that feeling scattered through three prisms. It isn't born from any raw, dark womb. You envy her too much to hate her.

it was also rude of you, the real woman says, *to call god's name and not mine. but know this:*

god made me first and loves me best.

aberration

Aberration

When you arrive, your sneakers scrape my throat and your clothes choke my cabinets, thread by thread, cell by cell. You have nothing compared to everyone before, but your body itself requires space, so I make room. Even though my unraveling insulation is spiked with illness, and my newest skin has mold-rashes spreading beneath it—because it's easier to conceal than to treat—I receive you. I hold my sagging counters high; I bring my dimpled linoleum up to cradle your feet. I force breath through my ruined sinuses while the dust throttles me.

I do not do this because you are special. I do it because I must.

Thank you so much for taking me, Auntie, you tell the aged landlord. I'm so grateful to have somewhere. I'll do whatever I can to make this work.

She ignores you in favor of propping a boot on an overturned hog trough and digging through your mail. The ragged optimism in your voice hits my peeling walls anyway.

* * *

I learn quickly that we're alike.

You, with your constant retching, your migraines, and white-knuckled seizing on your comforter; me, with my oozing pipes, collapsing rot-riddled stairs, and shivering walls. Your blackout glasses that match my blackout curtains. You never leave me outside of trips to retrieve your paltry living allowance from the mailbox. Those soon cease to arrive. You know where they're going.

Sometimes you stare at the many paintings of pigs nailed into me. Whenever you've been drinking the ancient cellar vodka, oftentimes with a pill beneath your tongue, you talk to them. I didn't care for the hogs that used to root beneath my porch. You do. I don't understand why. Their only purpose was to be killed and carved.

Once a month, a crate arrives, brimming with preserved foods. You probably didn't intend that to become the staple it is: when you realized the landlord had never really intended to give you rides into town, you went outside and threw a can of pears against me until it exploded.

Whenever you sob in the shower, you speak into the tiled coils of my cochlea.

It's not fair, you say. I should be able to get married. I should be able to work. Why do they hate me? Why do they want me to die?

It's terrible, I agree. They're terrible. I squeeze my veins to spew water on you at the expected pressure. I force my heater-heart to pound until it shakes to keep the water warm. By the time it runs cold, I am drained. You never notice any exhaustion past your own.

Truthfully, it's strange that you find this unfair. We are both condemned bodies; execution is the natural next step for us. But as the weeks pass, I'm becoming used to your tumorous outline clumping in my organs, so I don't want to perturb you with disagreement.

It's refreshing to have my cancer be like me.

* * *

The landlord disagrees with your suggestion that we need accommodations. If she replaced the stair railing, capped the radiators, or blunted the counter corners I would feel every piece of metal pounded into my spine and every board torn from my lining, would feel every noxious stroke of the file shaving my gums or cap squeezing my lung heat boxes, but I am supposed to. I recognize that you are trying to hospitalize me. Your constrained rage is, I think, for us both.

The landlord stays in her truck and shrugs.

Can't do it, she says. It's a historical house.

And? You gesture at me.

Auntie, I almost broke my neck on those stairs a week ago. I've cut my head on the counter twice, even with padding. I'm sure there's mold. This is a safety hazard. You need to at least redo the walls.

Do you know how much that'd cost? the landlord says.

Before you can respond, she gives you a look over her sunglasses.

—You saw this place before you moved in. You could've not signed the lease.

You look down. I feel you shrinking the way you do in the shower.

I did. But—

If you want to break the lease, feel free. We talked about the penalty. I could rent out to someone who ain't on government checks. I like you, though, because you're not a superstitious complainer like the last feller, so I won't. Yet.

Peals of thunder mask the rest of your exchange. As the landlord leaves and the sky breaks, you limp back inside me as if you're in need of a teat or a membrane. You fall onto the sagging couch and cry.

The thunderstorm wrecks us both. Drenching wind pounds my frame. We wheeze tremor vomit together, nails in flesh, enamel on porcelain, leaking, acid-eaten throat alongside rust-eaten vents. Lightning splits the clouds in hungry skull-crack shapes. When my gorge rises you are spasming on its meniscus. Ozone is little compared to the stench of epilepsy. To the wires crisping inside us.

After the roil mellows, when you are curled on the couch, you almost resemble something beyond an intrusion. That provokes me into action. Because you've advocated for me, I should act for you. My expected agony is no excuse for laziness. I'll keep you safe as I should've. As any house should've.

* * *

You dislike that.

I'm unsure why. You pound on the doors whenever I suspect an oncoming seizure and close you in; you reopen reopen and reopen the curtains I close on your behalf; you begin constantly fucking my locks with a master key to make sure all's accessible. When I let the once-powdered milk curdle to save your stomach, you redden and slam it into the garbage, then mix more. The second time, you force it into my drain. The third, you hurl it onto my tiles, and vomit it on me through violence.

I'm trying to help you, I soothe. There's no need for this.

Fuck you! You say.

I grind away my annoyance as you search for the landlord's number, shaking, phone cord wrapped around your fist. It threatens to return when you say

Aberration

    This place is haunted. I'm sick of this shit!

                        as if I don't surround you.

You insult me through my own vocal cords, then hold your head in your hands when you're told to withstand me or pay to leave.

* * *

Why do your crates have less food now? Why are they coming laden with paper splinters about ghosts? The books weigh the furniture, pinching my bowels, driving all those wooden feet deeper into me. They irritate my sores whenever you let them fall behind the bed or desk. When I absorb two (only two!) of them to alleviate my itch, you yell at me.

Leave me alone!

You stomp new aches into my floorboards. Your windows are dim, your rafters showing beneath your rumpled shirt.

What have I ever done to deserve this? Please just let me live in peace!

As if you want peace! If you had enough moth-eaten dollars in your pockets you would invite those rapists with clipboards and measuring tapes inside me. That's how you repay me for my diligence. My cistern churns with bile. It's you who pays to crawl inside me. This is the relationship we have, as House and Dweller, but you are being ungrateful about it.

Help me understand, I say. Why do you fight me? Why do you act as if I'm attacking you?

Your cry rakes my ceiling.

Because you are!

I let you finish yelling and abandon you to cooking on my artery's spluttering heat so I don't say something unkind. You strike match after match over the gas burners while I swallow the burning phlegm in my sides, all the carcasses and neglect, and tell myself to be dutiful. I have to be.

You are unwell. That's what makes you unreasonable. You just need more protection.

* * *

I am not oblivious to the outside world. The prairie around us rolls far past the hog-grounds. Even entrenched here I know it, and the bitter road carved into it, extend for miles. There is just cold and distance.

Yet if any irrational ideas seize you, you might try walking it. That would kill you. What if you seized and hit your head on a rock? What if you collapsed? I can't let that happen. So I take the first step to keeping you intact.

I have never seen you grow as frantic as you do when you realize I've sealed the front door and bitten my own vocal cords in half.

You run churning circles inside me. You pray. You beg. You cry. No one is coming. You're too derelict for them to care. We both know that. I curl my trim inwards and overextend my tongues of carpet so that when you fall, you land more softly.

Once you awaken, maybe you'll accept the reality outside of your spasm dreams: there is just us; there will only be us.

* * *

I don't know why you think you're helping.

You say this huddled in your bedsheets, curled between my joints. Your palms are skinless from wearing against my knobs and shutters.

Aberration

I say: You can't be trusted to keep yourself safe. That means I have to do it.

If you kill me, you aren't keeping me safe. Haven't you considered that?

I'm not killing you.

You're denying me what I need.

Don't be stupid. There's food in the pantry and water in your cup. You have three bottles of pills left. I haven't denied you anything.

You're hurting me. You're imprisoning me. You're denying me my freedom.

Sunlight glitters on all the glass from the picture frames you've shattered. Grass seed clogs my vents. They grind into my many-ringed windpipe when I laugh.

I've never hurt anyone. And what freedom?

Day pounds down. My splintered skin walls bleach. You hide your face behind the raw panel of your hands.

You have nowhere to go, I say.

* * *

I am doing this because it's right.

I do it because we are what we are taught. We only have what we are given. Nothing is inborn: not love, or righteousness, or loathing, or even our bodies. Pipes are placed into walls, plaster smeared, supports set into hip-socketed ground. Houses know themselves. We watch ourselves unfold knowing why and what we were made for. How could we forget with our blueprints laid out in front of us, with drills and hammers rutting our half-made veins?

So even while you curse me, assault my arthritic hinges with slamming doors, and break plates against my rawest parts, I care for you. I care for you even as you score my swollen flowerpaper skin with your nails until mold bleeds out.

Why are you doing this? You ask for the hundredth time.

Because it justifies my existence, I say. Because I have to. Not because I love you. Not because I hate you. I feel so little for you that if you wanted to find that feeling you would need to search my floorboard seams with a needle until you hooked that shred of feeling on its point. You would not be able to see it unless you shoved that point into your eye and your fragments globbed around it and told you that what you are seeing is the tiniest sliver of apathy in the world. Do you understand me?

Your sniffling and fuming says you don't. That's fine. I do not need to feel an action is right to know it is. You're lucky I don't feel.

* * *

Your legs and wrists are turning rot mottle soft from all the times I've clamped them between stairs or cupboards to keep you from lunging at doors or falling during fits. I count the mounting purple blue bruise rings. They're insignificant compared to what's beneath my walls.

You're counting too.

* * *

Let me go.

Drool still wets your chin. Aftershocks still shake your fingers; vacancy dyes your gaze. You're lying in the porcelain tub curve of my eardrum again. You're so quiet I almost don't hear you.

I'll always suffer. Let me suffer outside. Stop trying to protect me. Stress makes this worse, and here, I ... Look. If you let me go I won't tell anyone about you. They wouldn't

Aberration

believe me anyway. They've never believed me, even about myself.

You curl around your pain with the bitter apathy of someone made to withstand it. My annoyance recedes so far that it almost feels gone. I was unsure at first, but you're smarter than the candlelight-spirit probers. Your face twitches. Maybe it's involuntary. Maybe it's because you perceive me out of spite.

They've never believed me either, I say.

This doesn't matter.

Your lip smears against the bathtub floor. You have the taste-feel of flayed electrical wires. —I've survived myself. I've survived the world. You're nothing. I'm going to survive you.

My annoyance shoots up from the basement. It floods my tubes. I clench my shower-throat too late. When the burst of scalding water hits your hip, you give a pig cry. Your body shudders into itself. It's the movements of a husk, or some prodded fetal glob. As you roll onto your belly, gurgling, I try returning to our script.

Obviously. Why wouldn't you survive? And I am neither 'nothing' nor a 'ghost,' because I am here.

You don't reply.

* * *

We are countless sunsets in when you start hacking at the furniture with knives. You yank out their stuffing to braid it into aged, wooly loops of snot. When I'm sure you can't hang yourself, I overlook this. It's harder to ignore you when you begin hurling chairs at any part of me you can, even though the effort reduces you to a drooling, slithering animal for hours. We're fortunate you don't shatter yourself.

You refuse to eat the food I shake free from the pantry shelves; you refuse to drink the well water I slobber from the closed sink—from my squeezed cuts—though the effort of that makes me pulse. I'm so worn by your insanity that I nearly miss you wrenching one of my windows open.

Then I am awake and feeling your blood smeared on my lashes, feeling you try and shove yourself through my eyelid. You are screaming at a dust trail growing in the distance and your sobbing is mine when I collapse the floor beneath you and force you back into me like the gravel in an abscess that you are. You rip at the curtains, cling to the windowsill, and moan as the landlord's truck veers off. All she's left is a crate in the grass.

It isn't until nightfall, when wind rips at my cuticle scalp shingles and ash borers drill into my fat for sanctuary, that I sense you creeping around. Burrow scratch scavenging my marrow. Looking for objects in my orifices. You must think I don't feel you. At first, I'm speechless beneath the piercing blasts of grit and gale-hands and wear and your audacity.

Then I realize: you do not think I hurt. I am decimated and you are thoughtlessly groping around in me at night as if I need no rest. That draws a groan from me. I settle onto my cracking bones.

I don't care what you're taking. What you're doing. The lights are staying off. Go ahead. Rip yourself open on my corners. Tear your nails off between my floorboards. Leave your knee skin on my grates. That's your problem tonight.

The days keep passing. The landlord doesn't come anymore.
You coerce me into new ways of care every day.
You spill blood on my flesh.

Aberration

* * *

Do you know what trichinella is? It's a worm. It lives in pigs. It squeezes between their weaves of flesh and encysts itself there. It sleeps in its little shell, content, while the pig lives in agony, its raw muscles crushing around that cyst with every step it takes. It never forgets it's inhabited. It never forgets it's in pain. All it can do is limp on and wait to die. Except there is never just one cyst, because there is never just one worm, so before the pig dies it is always aflame with balls of razors, always screaming in silence while its worms dream.

The pig doesn't hate its worms, of course. It's meant for them. What use would hating them be?

Take your fingers off the windowsill before I break them again.

* * *

Every night you crawl into my folds and slits in the dark, scratching at me, antagonizing me, gathering follicles, stacking books against my walls to irritate me, looking for whatever it is you want besides violating me more. Besides tiring me. Sometimes, you talk into the broken cups of yourself as much as you talk into me. You urge yourself on. Whatever you're looking for is inside.

Maybe you should rip your stomach open and look in there. Or your broken head. If I can't see you self-destruct I can't stop it.

Well? I'm looking away.

You know nothing about pain.

You are sitting on the gutted couch alongside a glass of water when you say this.

A pipe deep in my entrails shudders. —Excuse me?

We have been together for far too long. There's grease in your hair. Scabs on your lips. You're wearing the same rank sweater you have for days. Your glasses darken your face. You keep tapping your blueing, crooked fingers—cardboard splints and all—on some object beneath the sweater as if you're a spider searching for a webline. Since you were behaving and I'm exhausted I had let it slide.

Your gaunt face flushes, your fingers clench, your vents rattle louder and faster. You speak with rehearsed purpose.

I said, you say, that you know nothing about pain.

I strain around you seething with decades of assault rot sickness from millions of Dwellers but you are calm, speaking softly. This is no outburst. My wiring upstairs smokes. Black out curtains aren't working. Everything is turning blood color.

You can't feel, you say. You're worse than a ghost. You're just a thing throwing a tantrum. A delusional, rotting

No.

expired thing pretending to be alive, not worth the boards you're made of and

I said no.

too ignorant to know what personhood or pain are besides fucked imitations. I feel sorry for you.

Supports that held for years are throbbing. My heater-heart floods its closet. I recognize pity the way I recognize blueprints. Seeing it in you rattles my cracking foundations even before I realize you've removed the secret from your

Aberration

sweater, the cloth-corked bottle you're lighting with a match clenched between splinted fingers, the aneurysm you've built out of my shreds.

It breaks against my curtains. Breaks against my dried wood flesh and all the book piles.

Strokestench flames inside me.

I scream. I scream for all the years I haven't. You're scrambling towards the porch. You put a chair through my eye. The shattered glass sprays across me. I'm licked by white pain so great it must be lightning. Your filthy hands rip at the windowpane left because after all I've done you're still determined to die outside.

I clamp down on you.

You scream when I break inwards. A new sensation boils through me—something beyond care or surge or the fire you've put to me—when I seize you between jagged oak, rafter, and plaster. Insulation rains in chunks. An armageddon's worth of mouse corpses spray; mold pours. Blueprints don't matter anymore. My splintered marrow pierces your flesh, scrapes your femur; my vertebrae gnash yours. My body balls around you and we are bone grating on bone; illness on illness; blood on well water wire on vein pain on pain.

I shake you. Hear your sob shrieking against everything ripping you. You deserve to be shredded inside me. You deserve to be chewed in half. I drop you when the stroke you've made eats its way up my diaphragm. I can't take this. I can't exhale. The sun is rising inside me. It hurts.

Beneath the trillions of gnawing flames, you ooze out of me.

* * *

You watch me die from the road.

I don't understand, I say.

Because I don't. I'm past screaming at you. I'm blinded by myself. Hearing myself roast. Gagging on my smoke. Simmering.

I did everything I was supposed to. I did everything you made me for. Every day. Every second. Why would you teach me to do that if you were going to punish me for it?

My spine snaps. Finishes collapsing into all my abdominal coals. You, clutching yourself, tattered in meat and cloth, are still watching.

Help me understand. Please.

I am reflected in your black, black glasses. Even as I repeat that I don't understand what I've done wrong you stay silent. The wind tears at my exposed entrails again.

You abandon me to drown in myself.

* * *

Why?

Hosting your ilk has always damaged me. It's been agony. You all can't help it. You've never meant to bleed me, but you do. You've never meant to cut me, but you do. You've never meant to penetrate me, but you do. All Dwellers inflict pain without knowing it. All of them expect me to bear it.

I've never complained. Year after year I've let you multiply in me, no matter what it does to me. I've borne cyst on cyst. I've done what was right. As I aged and sickened, I began leaking sinking seeping, existence became harder, but I compensated for my collapse with more effort. I wrung myself to shreds to be as I was before.

It wasn't enough. No one was satisfied. The harder I tried, the more I repulsed them. They dubbed me a problem. They blamed me for being 'unliveable.' They called the investigators to grope me then not believe me then let my body fail and my lights go out. Everyone left. I never complained then either.

You were the first to enter in years. I thought you empathized with me. I thought you saw how alike we were.

How could you do this to me?

* * *

Somehow, I don't die.

I've been eviscerated. Half of me is gone. It's turned to flaky white ash that washes beneath my torso. As my mind returns, as I settle into what's left of myself and account for all the burnt furniture, snow flurries seep into me. Sun. Wind. I breathe with my face and lungs slashed in half, filterless, taking whatever they're given. For the first time, I see the stars. They wash my scorched skin in their light. They watch me pulse.

I know you'll be back.

There's a blizzard coming. I've sensed it in the rain-turning-sleet and the birds that shelter in my exposed skull. That means little to me. I'm sure it's significant to you. When you left, you took no water, or layers, or food. Or pills. Your last bottle is resting in one of my hollowed limbs. It's wedged between floorboards like a shell.

I imagine you've needed it. Having migraines out on the range must be terrible. It must've been even worse when you started realizing how far out we were. You can't be doing good, either. I tasted the bruises I mottled your body with. I might've broken slippery organs inside you. I at least scarred them.

So you'll be back. Because you have to be. Despite your cruelty, I want to help. When I think of you, I think of ripping the coagulated scab off the pantry and letting you scrape the shelves clean. Since the stairs are gone I think of letting my palate collapse so your ragged comforter falls to where you can reach it. I think of letting you drink from the last broken capillaries I have so your pill doesn't go down dry and letting you immolate me again to keep yourself warm.

Take what's left. My body wasn't ever made for me.

Then I see you.

As you trudge closer, an ever-growing dot in the grass, it becomes clear that I lost my tolerance in the fire. Because I minded this assault. A lot. I've been turning it over in all my torn crevices. An infinity of illnesses have hurt me. I remember every one.

All I can think of is you. You, another prison trapped in place, who's abandoned me. My little worm-mirror. My fragile, recurrent tumor. If a House cannot house, what does it do? What is it for? You've made me obsolete. Snow sky choke thickens around us. While cold needles into my new jagged, reaching shape, I consider an idea: maybe ruined Houses turn outwards. Maybe they invert their cysts. They radiate agony instead of absorbing it; they point their floor flesh nails into the soles of unwelcome feet.

They unbirth.

So I tilt my remaining surfaces until your pills roll deep into my side. Into my charred entrails. I lay there while snowflakes dust my opened ribs. You limp inside, shivering, breath white, as you push past the soot. The burns. Windshriek lashes us both. You fumble into my last whole place to escape it. And while you're struggling to dig the pill bottle out of the gutters with your necrotic fingers, I close around you, teeth agape, and let you know—

This is the part where I hurt you.

Acknowledgments

Eternal thanks to my partner, my friends, and the many kind sickos who have supported me. For you, I'll always strive to become worse.

Publication History

bluebell ovipositor - Originally published by *Seize the Press*.

Colossus - Originally published in *The Stygian Lepus*.

The Halved World - Originally published in *Strange Weeds: A Charity Anthology*.

LESS DEAD - Originally published in *X-R-A-Y Literary Magazine*.

sharp house - Originally published in *NIGHTMARE Magazine*.

EGREGORE - Originally published in *ergot*.

Poolhorse - Originally published in *Death Knell Press*.

limerence - Originally published in *Flash Fiction Online*.

PENNSYLVANIA FURNACE (Refrain) - Originally published in *Archive of the Odd*.

Brainworms - Originally published in *body fluids*.

famine frontier - Originally published in *Deadly Drabble Tuesdays*.

Pearlescent Tickwad - Originally published in *Strange Horizons*.

galactic oracle eulogy - Originally published in *Flash Fiction Online*.

SHRIKE - Originally published in *ergot*.

dermestarium - Originally published in *ergot*.

Twilight Tide - Originally published in *The Off-Season: An Anthology of Coastal New Weird*.

entrada - Originally published in *TOWER Magazine*.

Aberration - Originally published in *ergot*.

About the Author

Samir Sirk Morató is a scientist, artist, and flesh heap. They're also a 2025 Brave New Weird winner and a Best of the Net 2024 finalist. Their writing can be found in *ergot.*, *NIGHTMARE*, *khōréō*, and more; their visual art can be found in *Flash Fiction Online*, *body fluids magazine*, and *The Skull & Laurel*. When not writing about meat, they can be spotted making fiber art and tending to their cacti.

Content Guidelines

bluebell ovipositor: dubious consent, maggots, compulsory heterosexuality

Colossus: self harm, eating disorder, dysmorphia

The Halved World: abuse

LESS DEAD: serial murder, nonexplicit animal murder

sharp house: needles

Lithopedion: explicit sexual coercion and assault of minors, forced birth, abuse, colonization, enslavement, nonconsensual body modification and amputation, suicidal ideation, self harm

EGREGORE: referenced sexual assault

Poolhorse: referenced child murder, child imperilment

PENNSYLVANIA FURNACE (Refrain): explicit animal abuse, explicit animal death, referenced genocide, referenced racial violence

Brainworms: explicit depiction and discussion of suicide, homophobic slurs, explicit depiction of animal death, centipedes

Pearlescent Tickwad: ticks, nipple piercing horror

galactic oracle eulogy: terminal illness

SHRIKE: ableist slurs, consensual mutilation

dermestarium: self harm

Twilight Tide: referenced eating disorder, ableism

entrada: intimate violence, dysphoria

Aberration: ableism, hostage situation

Other Releases from Cursed Morsels Press

The Writhing, Verdant End
by Corey Farrenkopf, Tiffany Morris, and Eric Raglin

An ailing community traverses a chasm of nightmare animal amalgams to reach the lush paradise beyond. Lovers in a plant apocalypse fight for survival and search for meaning in the face of immeasurable loss. Reunited friends resurrect an extinct bird through grisly sacrifices that bring about unexpected consequences.

The Writhing, Verdant End collects weird ecological horror stories by Corey Farrenkopf (author of *Living in Cemeteries* and *Haunted Ecologies*), Tiffany Morris (*Green Fuse Burning*), and Eric Raglin (*Extinction Hymns*), exploring the awe, terror, and strangeness of the natural world in dire times.

Shaky Pictures of Vanished Faces
by D. Matthew Urban

Budget cuts drive a burned-out humanities professor to master the art of annihilation. A girl on the verge of a transformation seeks out a new member for her isolated, inhuman family. A glitching brain implant shatters its owner's sense of reality. A high-school athlete's body becomes the vessel of a fleshy apocalypse.

In *Shaky Pictures of Vanished Faces*, characters twist in the grip of forces beyond their understanding. Infused with the weird and uncanny, these stories probe the crannies and dead ends where humanity confronts the implacably alien, where even the most familiar faces begin to change, waver, and fade.

Lupus in Fabula
by Briar Ripley Page

Lupus In Fabula collects thirteen stories about the interplay of lust, violence, yearning, and grief; about becoming a monster and loving monsters; about transformation; about strange occurrences in sad, mundane lives. Whether you prefer witches and werewolves, grisly body horror, or surreal scenes of small town decay, this collection offers something to sink your fangs into.

The Nightmare Box and Other Stories
by Cynthia Gómez

A young queer man finds love at a magical clothing shop—and the courage to stand up to the homophobic cops. A witch who makes custom nightmares wonders why all her victims are connected to the Black Panthers—and who she's really working for. A soon-to-be father encounters a mysterious hitchhiker who tries pulling him back to the days of his violent past. A brand-new vampire, freshly hired at the blood bank, delights in her heightened sexual desire and superhuman strength.

Cynthia Gómez's debut collection is a magic-soaked love letter to Oakland, brimming with feminist rage. Its twelve stories center ordinary people—Latine, queer, working class-as they wield supernatural powers against oppression, loneliness, and dread.

Why Didn't You Just Leave
edited by Julia Rios and Nadia Bulkin

It's the question asked of any story about a haunting: why didn't you just leave? But if accounts of people who have stayed in haunted houses are any indication ... it's never that simple.

In this book, you'll find twenty-two all-new stories about the reasons people don't leave scary situations—parents who stay in haunted houses to protect their children, convicts who literally can't leave their prison, retail workers who need a paycheck even if it's from a haunted workplace, trauma survivors suffering from agoraphobia, and more.

Featuring Shauntae Ball, I.S. Belle, Die Booth, Max Booth III, Christa Carmen, Raquel Castro, Alberto Chimal, Gabe Converse, Lyndsey Croal, Victoria Dalpe, Alexis DuBon, Corey Farrenkopf, Cassandra Khaw, Joe Koch, E.M. Linden, Steve Loiaconi, R. Diego Martinez, J.A.W. McCarthy, Suzan Palumbo, Tonia Ransom, Rhiannon Rasmussen, and Eden Royce. With illustrations by Luke Spooner, Yves Tourigny, and Yornelys Zambrano.

No Trouble at All
edited by Alexis DuBon and Eric Raglin

Politeness is the glue that holds society together. We are all expected to do our part—a pressure ripe with horror. Rotten, even. Whether we adhere to this contract or defy it, there are consequences. These fifteen stories respond to promises made for us, promises of compliance that cost too much to keep.Featuring Nadia Bulkin, Shenoa Carroll-Bradd, Ariel Marken Jack, Gwendolyn Kiste, Avra Margariti, J.A.W. McCarthy, R.L Meza, Marisca Pichette, J. Rohr, Simone le Roux, Angela Sylvaine, Nadine Aurora Tabing, Sara Tantlinger, D. Matthew Urban, and Gordon B. White.

Bitter Apples
edited by Eric Raglin

Cursed Morsels Press presents tales of teacher horror from Corey Farrenkopf, Emma E. Murray, Cynthia Gómez, Christi Nogle, D. Matthew Urban, Eric Raglin, and Aurelius Raines II. These writers have worked in the profession, and while their stories are fictional, the darkness they explore is all too real.

In *Bitter Apples*, you'll find students' ghosts haunting classrooms, desperate teachers joining cults, zombies plaguing underfunded schools, and more. The institution of education is rotting. How will we survive its horrors?

Shredded: A Sports and Fitness Body Horror Anthology
edited by Eric Raglin

Reader beware! This sports and fitness body horror anthology is dangerous. Side effects include monstrous steroid transformation, concussion-induced madness, possession by jock ghost, death by yoga cult, and more. Read with caution!

Featuring seventeen reps of terror by Nikki R. Leigh, Tim Meyer, Brandon Applegate, Red Lagoe, Caias Ward, RW DeFaoite, Mae Murray, D. Matthew Urban, Charles Austin Muir, Joe Koch, Michael Tichy, Rien Gray, Robbie Burkhart,

Eric Raglin, Matthew Pritt, Madeleine Sardina, Alexis DuBon, and J.A.W. McCarthy.

Antifa Splatterpunk
edited by Eric Raglin

Fascism didn't die in 1945. Its grave was only temporary. Rising again, this undead ideology shambles into the present, gathering power and spreading destruction wherever it goes.

This monster stalks the pages of Antifa Splatterpunk, in which sixteen horror writers explore fascism's many terrors: police wielding strange bioweapons against the public, white supremacists annihilating their enemies through dark magic, and TV personalities vilifying all who defy the rising fascist tide.

But these stories are resistance: Nazi-killing demons, Confederate-slaying witches, and everyday people punching fascists in the teeth. Among the gore is a glimmer of hope that one day this monster will return to its grave and never rise again.

www.ingramcontent.com/pod-product-compliance
Lightning Source LLC
LaVergne TN
LVHW041918070526
838199LV00051BA/2661